PRAISE FOR M.

Buchman has catapulted his way to the top tier of my favorite authors.

— FRESH FICTION

Nonstop action that will keep readers on the edge of their seats.

— *TAKE OVER AT MIDNIGHT,* LIBRARY JOURNAL

M L. Buchman's ability to keep the reader right in the middle of the action is amazing.

— LONG AND SHORT REVIEWS

The only thing you'll ask yourself is, "When does the next one come out?"

— *WAIT UNTIL MIDNIGHT,* RT REVIEWS, 4 STARS

The first…of (a) stellar, long-running (military) romantic suspense series.

— *THE NIGHT IS MINE,* BOOKLIST, “THE 20 BEST ROMANTIC SUSPENSE NOVELS: MODERN MASTERPIECES”

I knew the books would be good, but I didn’t realize how good.

— NIGHT STALKERS SERIES, KIRKUS REVIEWS

Buchman mixes adrenalin-spiking battles and brusque military jargon with a sensitive approach.

— PUBLISHERS WEEKLY

13 times “Top Pick of the Month”

— NIGHT OWL REVIEWS

Tom Clancy fans open to a strong female lead will clamor for more.

— *DRONE,* PUBLISHERS WEEKLY

Superb!

— *DRONE,* BOOKLIST STARRED REVIEW

The best military thriller I've read in a very long time. Love the female characters.

— *DRONE,* SHELDON MCARTHUR, FOUNDER OF THE MYSTERY BOOKSTORE, LA

A fabulous soaring thriller.

— *TAKE OVER AT MIDNIGHT,* MIDWEST BOOK REVIEW

Meticulously researched, hard-hitting, and suspenseful.

— *PURE HEAT,* PUBLISHERS WEEKLY, STARRED REVIEW

Expert technical details abound, as do realistic military missions with superb imagery that will have readers feeling as if they are right there in the midst and on the edges of their seats.

— *LIGHT UP THE NIGHT,* RT REVIEWS, 4 1/2 STARS

AT THE MEREST GLANCE

A PARANORMAL ROMANTIC SUSPENSE

M. L. BUCHMAN

Buchman Bookworks

Published by Buchman Bookworks, Inc.

Receive a free book and discover more by this author at: www.mlbuchman.com

Cover images:

3D Golden Greek Letter Psi © georgios | Depositphotos

Blue Water © Arena Creative | Depositphotos

SIGN UP FOR M. L. BUCHMAN'S NEWSLETTER TODAY

and receive:
Release News
Free Short Stories
a Free Book

Get your free book today. Do it now.
free-book.mlbuchman.com

Other works by M. L. Buchman: (* - also in audio)

Thrillers

Dead Chef

Swap Out!
One Chef!
Two Chef!

Miranda Chase

*Drone**
*Thunderbolt**
*Condor**

Romantic Suspense

Delta Force

*Target Engaged**
*Heart Strike**
*Wild Justice**
*Midnight Trust**

Firehawks

MAIN FLIGHT

Pure Heat
Full Blaze
*Hot Point**
*Flash of Fire**
Wild Fire

SMOKEJUMPERS

*Wildfire at Dawn**
*Wildfire at Larch Creek**
*Wildfire on the Skagit**

The Night Stalkers

MAIN FLIGHT

The Night Is Mine
I Own the Dawn
Wait Until Dark
Take Over at Midnight
Light Up the Night
Bring On the Dusk
By Break of Day

AND THE NAVY

Christmas at Steel Beach
Christmas at Peleliu Cove

WHITE HOUSE HOLIDAY

*Daniel's Christmas**
*Frank's Independence Day**
*Peter's Christmas**
*Zachary's Christmas**
*Roy's Independence Day**
*Damien's Christmas**

5E

Target of the Heart
Target Lock on Love
Target of Mine
Target of One's Own

Shadow Force: Psi

*At the Slightest Sound**
*At the Quietest Word**

White House Protection Force

*Off the Leash**
*On Your Mark**
*In the Weeds**

Contemporary Romance

Eagle Cove

Return to Eagle Cove
Recipe for Eagle Cove
Longing for Eagle Cove
Keepsake for Eagle Cove

Henderson's Ranch

*Nathan's Big Sky**
*Big Sky, Loyal Heart**
*Big Sky Dog Whisperer**

Love Abroad

Heart of the Cotswolds: England
Path of Love: Cinque Terre, Italy

Other works by M. L. Buchman:

Contemporary Romance (cont)

Where Dreams

Where Dreams are Born
Where Dreams Reside
Where Dreams Are of Christmas
Where Dreams Unfold
Where Dreams Are Written

Science Fiction / Fantasy

Deities Anonymous

Cookbook from Hell: Reheated
Saviors 101

Single Titles

The Nara Reaction
Monk's Maze
the Me and Elsie Chronicles

Non-Fiction

Strategies for Success

Managing Your Inner Artist/Writer
*Estate Planning for Authors**
Character Voice
*Narrate and Record Your Own Audiobook**

Short Story Series by M. L. Buchman:

Romantic Suspense

Delta Force

Delta Force

Firehawks

The Firehawks Lookouts
The Firehawks Hotshots
The Firebirds

The Night Stalkers

The Night Stalkers
The Night Stalkers 5E
The Night Stalkers CSAR
The Night Stalkers Wedding Stories

US Coast Guard

US Coast Guard

White House Protection Force

White House Protection Force

Contemporary Romance

Eagle Cove

Eagle Cove

Henderson's Ranch

*Henderson's Ranch**

Where Dreams

Where Dreams

Thrillers

Dead Chef

Dead Chef

Science Fiction / Fantasy

Deities Anonymous

Deities Anonymous

Other

The Future Night Stalkers
Single Titles

ABOUT THIS BOOK

Army helicopter pilot Anton Bowman *could always see more than everyone else. Even as a kid, he could send his vision out to look around in places his body hadn't actually gone.*

Katie Whitfield *embraces her lonely status as an outsider. Her livelihood as a wildlife tracker across the English countryside keeps her content and well clear of her uncaring family.*

Both their lives change when the gifted members of the Shadow Force: Psi team travel to England as part of a security test. A test that uncovers unexpected dangers to both the UK's network of undersea cables and to their hearts.

CHAPTER 1

Seven steps.

Six.

Five.

Anton felt as if he was climbing to the gallows.

At the head of the stairs, he cracked his forehead on the doorframe to his room. As Ma used to say, "Probably knocked more sense outta ya than inta ya."

"Sure thing, Ma."

And he'd remembered to duck for this one. It was just that doors in a five-hundred-year-old Cornish inn were even lower than most. Old houses, like his parent's North Carolina farmhouse, were a real problem for a guy who was six-five. He'd cracked his head on the back kitchen door so many times that Pa had nailed a doubled strip of old blanket on both sides because he never seemed to learn.

Anton collapsed kitty-corner onto the bed and groaned.

Despite all his years flying for the Army, jet lag always

kicked his ass, and this trip had been no different. Besides, when he was flying a helo, he wasn't jaunting through six time zones in a single day. But good old San Antonio, Texas, now lay a quarter of the world away.

On top of that, dudes his size were not designed to be folded up into airplanes for twelve hours.

Just to continue his losing streak, he'd lost the front-seat toss for the five-hour drive from London to Cornwall. Of course, that was kind of a given, as Jesse's wife Hannah was the best driver the team had, so the cowboy always claimed the navigator seat. Watching the crazed English drivers race by on the wrong side of roads so narrow that they barely deserved the name, Anton had almost been glad to be in the back with the rest of the team.

It wasn't even coming up dusk yet, but he didn't care. They'd eaten something he didn't remember in the inn's pub, and now he could just stretch out and pray that his body recovered sometime this decade.

Seven p.m. local meant it was only one in the afternoon in San Antonio, so his mind was wide awake. Or was it one in the morning?

Didn't know. Didn't care.

With nothing left to do but ache, Anton decided it was time to put himself back on the winning side of the coin. And, at that moment, that meant the best place to be was anywhere else, so he went "lookabout."

His semi-sister always called it "going walkabout" like in that Australian movie she'd watched when they were kids. But it was *his* vision, so it was "lookabout" no matter what she said.

He closed his eyes and let his personal, private magic trick slip out of the room—his out-of-body vision went sightseeing while his body lay there unkinking.

Anton mentally strolled his vision through the closed door, down the stairs, and peeked in on the rest of the Shadow Force: Psi team. Yep, they were still downstairs in the pub. They'd claimed they were going exploring through the town, and the April evening was nice enough for it, but not a one had moved so much as a muscle. Lame-os.

He hadn't been in the mood to really notice earlier, but the pub looked majorly cozy, old-style Cornwall.

He had to laugh; his semi-sister Michelle was leaning half asleep against Ricardo. It was still weird thinking of them as a couple, but since they'd married last month and he'd stood as best man, he'd better get used to it. It had given him the oh-so-sweet opportunity to threaten Ricardo with utter mayhem if he made Michelle unhappy. Of course, based on growing up with her and being Ricardo's best man and all, he'd gotten to threaten Michelle with the same. Two for the price of one, which totally made it worth the price of admission.

The other three team members looked equally hammered. Easy bet he'd crashed only minutes before they would. Sure enough, Jesse and Hannah made excuses that Anton couldn't hear. He often wished that his hearing would go for a stroll with his vision, but it never did. Instead his ears were still back in the room listening to the occasional pop from his abused vertebrae.

The way they were holding hands as they headed for

the stairs, without seeing him, told him that they had other ideas about how to cure their jetlag. Must be nice.

One more flip to the wrong side of the coin; he hadn't found a lady to do the horizontal tango with in far too long.

He looked away to give them their privacy, because it so wasn't envy. Really not.

Only Isobel found her feet and headed out on a walk. She had on her winter jacket. Spring here in Cornwall was in the fifties, still colder than a San Antonio winter. Of course, April was already kicking out dailies over ninety back in Texas, so it was kind of a relief.

Anton followed her for a bit. The place had a harbor about the size of five Dixie cups. The town wrapped around it in a broad crescent, and a big granite seawall curled in from either side like a dragon's jaw. Cute as hell.

He lost Isobel in the evening light when he wasn't paying attention. How he did that with one of the most beautiful movie stars anywhere in a town as small as Mousehole, Cornwall, was a mystery, but he did.

Maw-zel he reminded himself. That's how the locals pronounced it, which was too bad. Mousehole was a good name and he'd have fought to fix that…if he was a local and not here on a secret mission. At its core, the town was pretty much three streets deep and ten very narrow blocks wide. It snugged up against a small harbor and a looming curved breakwater of neat-laid massive stone block.

But he didn't want to explore the town. If everything went according to plan, they'd be here for a week with plenty of time to poke around.

No, what he wanted to do was get a jump on Ricardo. If a guy couldn't get back at a guy for marrying his semi-sister, the least he could do was out-sneak him.

So, while Ricardo was probably escorting Michelle upstairs for a quick nap, or a slow tumble (which shit Anton definitely didn't want to be thinking about), he caught a ride out of town.

He couldn't move his out-of-body vision any faster than he could move his own body—which was a pain in the butt, except his butt was still back in a nice soft bed at the Ship Inn. With enough details, and if it wasn't too far away, he could jump to a place…with help. Photos didn't work; someone had to be describing it who was actually there. Once he'd been there, he could get back and pick up at that point, but only for a few hours. If he missed that window, he had to start all over again.

Lookabouts had been a very slow process until he'd figured out how to hitch a ride.

Anton found a car headed west out of town and slipped "aboard." It was faster than walking, mostly.

Everything was so damn green. San Antone was already cooking its way over to a soft tan, April just a prelude to the midsummer brown. Here it was like somebody'd dumped the entire US Army's supply of camo greens over the countryside. Everywhere he looked, something else was in bloom or growing up between other things. It reminded him of his parent's farm along the North Carolina shore. He missed that green sometimes. Didn't miss the farming much, but missed that look and smell of honeysuckle blooming on the night air.

After a while, the road offered tantalizing views of the

sunset sea—in microscopically brief flashes. Mostly it wove over rolling hills as a single lane pinched between towering hedges. Not that the traffic was one-way. These English drivers could actually pass each other with only a little hesitation, but that was because most of the cars were VWs or MINI Coopers.

The frequent Range Rovers caused some trouble.

But when a truck or bus came by, there simply wasn't enough room. Everyone slowed to a crawl, pushing into the hedges to get by.

For once he was glad that his hearing didn't come along for his travels. It was easy to imagine the sharp *scree* of hard-pressed branches scrubbing against paint. It explained why the entire passenger side of the rental SUV had been so scuffed up. In fact, most cars and trucks in Cornwall seemed to be messed up along the left side and now he knew why.

It took a couple of hops, but he made it the fifteen kilometers west to Sennen Cove in under an hour. He could have run it almost as fast, but it was strangely taxing to "run" his vision. He preferred to walk or ride.

He hopped off near the Land's End Airport. England ended just a kilometer or so down the road. Next stop, other than the Isles of Scilly, was the Bahamas. Wouldn't that be sweet. Stretched out on the beach with a long lady, their dark skin a sharp contrast to the white sand and turquoise water. But no. They were in the cool damp of an April evening in Cornwall. He could even feel it invading his room at the inn because he'd left the window open to the sea salt air.

From the airport where he hopped "off" the car, his

destination of Sennen Cove was a couple hundred meters across the countryside, but he didn't mind the walk at all. So different from wide prairie lands around San Antonio where the team was sort-of based. Once away from the hedged roads, the softly rolling land here had a comfortable openness with a surprising lushness.

After he'd "walked" across the middle of the runway, he was in Cornish farmland. Small fields with piled stone walls spread in every direction except for a little bunch of trees that looked so perfect that they might have been planted. England was even more tame than his parents' farm outside of Shallotte. Close by the sea and South Carolina, it felt closer to Cornwall than San Antonio.

After a decade of flying helos for the Army's 10th Mountain, and whatever strangeness the last year in San Antonio with Shadow Force: Psi had been, home was still the family farm. Especially at times like this. He missed it like a hole in his heart.

It was a beautiful night traveling through the Cornish countryside, but he could almost be walking the thick, warm nights back into the Green Swamp Preserve with Pa. Pa wasn't much of a talker, but their after-dinner strolls had been a fixture of his youth.

He shook his head to clear it, and almost lost the connection to himself. He was still stretched out at the Ship Inn along Mousehole's waterfront, but he'd rather be here.

Especially because he could pre-scout the mission before the others. That way he'd know more about what was what than Ricardo.

He was going to bypass the cluster of trees when he

spotted the heat signature of a pair of footsteps across the field. Much like his helicopter's night-vision gear, his lookabout vision expanded into the infrared.

The two sets of footprints sure weren't walking side-by-side like a couple of teenagers looking for privacy. In fact, they were single file, almost as if one was being driven unwillingly.

He thought of how he and his team had saved Ricardo's ass eighteen months ago—tied up and being tortured in a Honduran drug camp.

Yeah, definite detour time.

He shifted to a jog and followed the footsteps toward the trees.

Waiting is.

Katie Whitfield had to remind herself of that, especially with clients like this one. When she was on her own, it was never a problem. Waiting was a wilderness tracker's natural state. Even when the wilderness was the tame Cornish countryside.

Be still.

Observe.

Then be still some more.

Accept that the mind was the very slowest of all the senses.

Eyes, ears, smell, taste, touch all offered immediate information. But even a mind trained to the task took time to process that information and find the thread that didn't fit.

Tonight, the thread that didn't fit at all was the man lying on his stomach among the bluebells to her right and a pace behind. It was terribly distracting.

The quest was easy because she'd long since tracked their quarry to this copse of trees below the airport.

Badgers naturally paired with beech trees and bluebells. They all three liked dry, chalky soil. And badgers also liked steep banks that faced southwest.

What made this particular colony special was the presence in the clan of an erythristic badger with his rare rust-red coloring.

Chas Thorstad was the third wildlife photographer she'd led to the site in the last six months. *The Guardian,* BBC, and now this twit. Even the chap from *The Guardian* had more of a clue about how to handle his gear than Thorstad.

He moved quietly enough, unlike the first two photographers she'd led here, with all the woods-sense of a pair of humpback whales. But his gear far outclassed him. She liked the Sony a7S II and wouldn't mind having one if she had a couple thousand pounds lying around looking for something to do. However, his monster lens, which probably cost ten times more than the camera body, would be better suited for photographing small planets than badgers at close range.

Maybe it was spite, but she actually led him right to the edge of where, even a meter closer, they'd be disturbing the badgers. At this distance his lens would let him photograph their teeth or maybe just one tooth at a time.

He didn't complain. Or change lenses.

There was something off about him. But he hadn't quibbled over her fee—which had doubled as soon as she saw his equipment.

She eased out her night monocular, which had set her back a whole hundred pounds. It gave her a beautiful view of the badgers' sett—their home was clear beneath the low-hanging beech trees despite the late evening light. Seven thirty-centimeter holes had been dug back into the hillside. This was a good-sized clan of at least ten individuals, and their tunnels would penetrate as deep as eighty meters into the hillside.

A black-and-white triangular head popped up from a hole, glanced in their direction for a long moment, then went about its business. The evening hours in April were a busy time for badgers. It was nearing the peak of their mating season, which meant a lot of grooming, play, and sex. It was also when the cubs would first venture to the entrances. She made a mental note to come back next month when they began exploring beyond the tunnels under their parents' watchful eyes.

What was so special about this site was that the biggest boar…

"There," she whispered to Chas.

Weighing at least fifteen kilos, despite it only being spring, made him exceptionally large by badger standards. His face was red-and-white rather than black-and-white. His body was rusty rather than the normal gray.

He glared down at their position.

Perhaps she'd pushed them a little too close. The size of a small pit bull, a roused badger could be far more dangerous. Not only did it have a vicious bite, but its long claws could easily slice through clothes and flesh.

She held her breath for a long thirty seconds before he huffed at them, then turned left to greet one of the females. A pair of cubs plowed awkwardly into his side. He briefly played with them, then returned his attention to the female.

"Tell me you got that," she whispered to Chas.

"Uh, yeah," he spoke too loudly and the badgers scattered back into the sett's holes, herding the cubs ahead of them.

The big erythristic male glared at her one last time, perhaps debating between ducking out of sight versus coming down the slope to shred them up a bit. If it came after them, she would make bloody certain she outran Chas Thorstad. She had no problem throwing him to the wolves, or rather to the badgers, to secure her own escape.

The boar chose to duck out of sight.

Katie suspected that if she came here again, he'd pick up her scent and chase her off right away.

She should have tripled her bloody fee.

"Well, they won't be back for a while," she pushed up to her knees and turned.

"Doesn't matter. I have what I need." Again, he was holding his camera oddly, as if he'd been taking pictures of something else entirely.

"Good, then let's go." The sooner she was done with Chas Thorstad the happier she'd be. Halfway to her feet, she hesitated and looked around.

Something, like a guy staring at you across a pub, prickled over her skin.

Darkness.

She raised her night-vision monocular and scanned again.

Nothing.

There were only the two of them.

They started tramping back to her aging MINI Cooper parked by the beach at Sennen Cove.

But she couldn't get over the feeling that someone was watching her.

Ten meters down the trail, she hesitated. It felt as if someone was waiting—right in front of her.

Bracing herself, she walked forward and…the feeling was gone.

CHAPTER 2

The pounding on his door snapped Anton's mind back into his room at Ship Inn.

"What!"

He hadn't wanted to lose that vision.

Whoever she was made looking a real joy. But there was something more. The way she'd acted. Almost as if—

"Get your ass up, you lazy dog. If you fall asleep now, you'll be toast tomorrow." Michelle blew into the room like the whirlwind his semi-sister was. He was impressed that she'd knocked at all.

Michelle Bowman was five-ten of maddening redhead —her skin as light as his was dark. They had the same parents, kind of. Ma and Pa had married, divorced, then married other people. Each having a kid, which had then blown up both of their second marriages. So they'd gotten back together and remarried when both Anton and Michelle were three. Yet she insisted that they weren't stepsiblings. Her answer to what they were kept changing, but for now Michelle was his semi-sister.

Ricardo offered a quiet grimace of apology as he entered behind his wife.

What Anton wanted to do was go watch that woman in the woods some more.

It was hard to tell in the dark, but he was pretty sure that her hair, falling in a thick ragged cut down past her shoulders, was strawberry blonde. No more than five-seven to his six-five, her head had passed below his chin when she'd walked up to him on the trail. But it wasn't how fine she looked lying on the ground with her jeans tight around her that had captured his attention. Okay, not only that.

He'd liked watching her watch the badgers. Smooth and quiet. A stillness about her that his semi-sister would never understand. She—

"Up, up, you lazy sod," Michelle slapped a hand hard against his gut. His childhood's worth of training had his gut muscles already clenched in protection, but it still stung.

"Dammit, Missy. Can't you let a man rest in peace?"

"A man, sure. But you're not a man, you're my demi-brother."

"Demi-brother?" Despite knowing there was no hope for her going away, he kept lying there just to mess with her.

"Yep! Like not even worth paying full price for."

"You do know—" Anton turned to Ricardo. "She does know that I can still beat the shit out of her. Right?"

Ricardo held up his hands saying to leave him out of whatever mess this was. Hard to blame the guy. Anton had no idea how he did it. Couldn't pay him enough to be married to Michelle, even if she wasn't his demi-semi-whatever-sister. The woman had no idea what it meant to just chill. He supposed that it was the final proof that Delta Force operators were just way more patient than Army Black Hawk pilots.

"Now!" Michelle ground out at him.

Not wanting to get kicked by her Crayola-red cowboy boots, he shoved to his feet and went to stretch—banging his knuckles painfully on the low ceiling.

"Never learn, do you?" Michelle swung out the door and led them downstairs to the pub. He ducked to clear the door jamb and followed. The dinner crowd had faded into convivial groups chatting over a pint and a slice of apple pie or cheesecake.

"Now this is my kinda place." He'd been too lagged during dinner to really notice it. Hell, he couldn't even remember what calories he'd shoveled down a couple of hours ago.

The pub was a combo of ancient stone and a white-painted heavy-beam ceiling. The room narrowed toward one end until it held only one round table. Someone with a sense of humor had hung a big picture of the view from an old sailing ship's bowsprit at the wall behind the table. It definitely felt as if they were on a ship. A double handful of tables lined port and starboard of the room. The stern was a well-equipped bar with eight taps and an impressive little whiskey collection.

"Oh yeah," Ricardo agreed just loudly enough to be heard over the quiet conversations. No sports screens. No sea shanty group for the tourists. Just folks enjoying each other's company. More than half looked like locals, two with dogs asleep at their feet.

The table in the bowsprit end of the room opened up. Michelle had the wits to snag it even though others were open. There he could stretch out his legs without tripping up the waitress every time she went by.

Ricardo lagged behind to order the first round at the bar.

"You ready for tomorrow, Missy?" Anton asked after they sat.

"You ever going to stop calling me that?"

"Not as long as it pisses you off."

"It does."

"My point."

She sighed and leaned back in her chair. "Tomorrow? What do I know about submarine cables?"

"A lot less than you'll know in a couple days? Don't worry, I don't know shit about them either. That's Hannah and Ricardo's department." And…aw, crap. He'd gotten distracted by the fine blonde lying in the woods. In just an hour or so his connection to the place would have faded, and he'd have to retrace the whole damn route to go lookabout there. *Double crap on white bread!* No one-upping Ricardo tomorrow.

Ricardo showed up with three beers. He pushed a pale ale toward Michelle and took an amber for himself. He passed a stout to Anton.

Michelle looked down at it. "That beer's darker than you are, little brother." She might be seven inches shorter than he was, and about as big around as his thigh, but she'd been born to Ma ten days before he'd been born to Pa's in-between-wife, and had never let him forget it.

He held it up to the light and she was right. It was pitch black. "Good thing I got me such a sweet heart."

Michelle sneered happily and the three of them clinked their glasses together.

"You owe me the bloody fee and you know it." Katie had only one other client ever stiff her, a lawyer. "Are you a lawyer?"

"No, I'm a photographer."

"Well, whatever you are, you owe me my fee, Chas Thorstad." She thumped a fist on the Ship Inn's bar for emphasis.

"I don't have the money, Katie."

Katie wondered if it would be worth hitting a client, knowing it meant that she would *never* be paid. He was a good hand taller that she was and strong; if she hit him, it wasn't likely to turn out well. Of course, most of the folks in the Ship Inn pub knew her and—

Chas seemed to levitate into the air until his feet were dangling near her knees. She stepped back to avoid being kicked as he struggled.

"Lady says you owe her a fee, my friend." The voice behind Chas was deep and dangerously soft. "Seems to me she earned it."

Katie looked up, way up, to see the person holding Chas aloft by his jacket collar. He was a giant of black man. His white t-shirt said, "BBQ Pit" in dripping red-sauce letters. There wasn't an ounce of fat on him. His biceps barely seemed to bulge as he held Chas aloft.

Chas aimed a vicious elbow strike behind him, which didn't work well with his jacket pinning his arms. It didn't matter as it bounced off the giant's shoulder.

The giant shook him once—hard.

Chas stopped struggling.

Still not setting him down, he reached out Chas' wallet and handed it over. "How much does he owe you?"

She opened the wallet and riffled through the thick wad of pound notes. Screw it! She took her *triple* fee, then handed the wallet back. That would pay rent on her room for next month.

The giant stuffed it back into Chas' pocket, then tossed him negligently aside. His aim was perfect.

In midflight, Chas squeaked in panic. Then he slammed against the front door and tumbled out into the street. A brief salty wind blew in from the harbor. Then Clive, still smelling of his day working the fish nets, shut the door and muttered, "Eejit. What a tuss."

"You okay?" Then the giant looked down at her and his eyes went wide. "Holy shit!"

Katie knew she wasn't the sort of woman that men said such things about.

Still, he kept staring.

"Do I know you?" She'd meant to thank him for his help, but he was somehow familiar. Not that she'd ever seen him before. There was no possibility of forgetting such a man.

"Yes. No. I know..." He stumbled over his words, shook his head like a wet terrier, then tried again. "I *definitely*...uh, would remember you." His words didn't sound quite truthful. The first part was okay, it sounded like a sincere compliment. But there was something gone awry in the latter part of that short sentence.

His familiarity bothered her. It was recent. Not the sight of him, but the...feel of him? Now she was getting into her best friend's Earth-Mother interconnected-universe crap. Dora would already be going on about souls meeting and—

"Uh, look. Glad I was able to help. If you want to join us, me, my friends..." he nodded toward a couple at the bowsprit table. "Well, anyway. It's a pleasure to actually... uh...meet you in person."

"In person compared to what?"

He looked at her wild-eyed, grunted something, then picked up the three pints James had pulled for him and hustled off to his table.

She picked up her own pint of Mena Dhu "Black Hill" stout, and tossed James a fiver from her new-found wealth. She took a sip and let the toasted, dark-chocolate taste roll across her tongue.

The giant *was* familiar. Recently, like...this evening.

However, it had been only her and Chas out at the badger sett.

She chatted with James long enough to find out about Tabby's newest attempts to take her first steps. His little girl was apparently furious that her body couldn't yet do what her brain could already picture.

Then she turned, and down the length of the room the big guy was looking right at her over the rim of his glass of the same stout she was drinking. He snorted his swallow, choked, and the tall redhead leaned over to pound him on the back with an easy familiarity—though none too gently. Then she leaned against his shoulder obviously teasing him about something.

Katie knew that she didn't have much power over men. Definitely not like his redheaded companion must wield. She'd been fairly sure that he'd been flirting with her, if doing an even worse job of that than she would have. Why would he do that when he was obviously so close to the stunning redhead?

Still, the fact that Katie was able to completely discomfit him, and that he'd helped her get paid, led her to nod thoughtfully to the end of James' story, then stroll down to the table.

"You the one upsetting Anton?" The redhead asked by way of introduction.

"Apparently."

A holly-berry red cowboy boot shoved out the closest chair. "You just gotta join us. Always glad to meet someone who can mess with my demi-brother's head. I'm Michelle. This quiet boyo, he's Ricardo." She leaned over and kissed him on the temple in a way that clearly stated, "This one is mine," without appearing to be rude about it.

Ricardo, a sleek Hispanic, tipped his beer glass to her in acknowledgement, then swept it ever so slightly toward the empty chair. Which still didn't explain what the redhead was to Anton.

"*Demi*-brother?" Katie sat before she had a chance to really think it through.

"No, don't—" Anton started, but then yelped. Katie had

the distinct impression that Michelle had just kicked his shin under the table with the toe of those red boots.

"Okay, *demi* is too much. What's less than half?"

Anton was still watching her a bit wildly. It was getting a little unnerving.

"Less than a demi?" Katie sipped her beer slowly to draw out the moment. "How about a dram-brother?"

"Like a dram of whiskey. How much is that?"

"A dram is an eighth of an ounce."

"An eighth of a—" Michelle squealed. "That's perfect! Everyone, raise your glass." When they all had, she announced loudly enough for the entire pub to overhear. "To my dram-brother and the woman who messes with his head."

They all clinked glasses, even Anton, and drank to the toast.

He didn't appear the least put out by Michelle's declaration of his unimportance.

"Step-sibs," Ricardo spoke for the first time.

"Dram-sibs!" Michelle turned on him ready for a fight. "We're nowhere *near* step-sibs. Thank God!"

His response was to cup her cheek and kiss her very soundly. A choice that softened the hard-edged woman with a surprising abruptness.

"Newlyweds," Anton whispered in that lovely deep voice of his. His affection for both of the others clear in his tone.

Now she knew where he was familiar from. "Tonight. You were…" But that was impossible. It had been only her, Chas, and the badgers. Yet, somehow, he'd been there.

When she tried to look into his eyes, his gaze slid aside too fast.

"You *were* there. How? I didn't see you."

"Hey," Michelle reentered the conversation by slapping her dram-brother on his shoulder. "Is that what you were doing earlier?"

"Missy," Anton growled at her.

"Michelle," Ricardo's soft admonishment brought brilliant color to Michelle's cheeks.

"Uh, don't mind me." Then she concentrated on playing with her beer glass though her cheeks continued to flame as brightly as her hair.

"How were you there and not there?" Katie turned back to Anton. The group had shifted from fun to suddenly tense in ways that she didn't like one bit.

"How did you know I was? Uh, I wasn't…" Anton struggled.

Katie pushed to her feet. She didn't need these people. Didn't want to know any more about—

When she turned to leave, she almost plowed down a beautiful woman only a few centimeters shorter than she was.

No, not just some beautiful woman. This was one of Hollywood's hottest rising stars, Isobel Manella.

"Holy shit!" She couldn't think of what else to say. She'd never met a famous person before in her life. Now she knew exactly how Anton had felt the first time he'd looked at her by the bar. Though for the life of her she still couldn't imagine why.

CHAPTER 3

"Isn't this all just so interesting?" Isobel's smooth Latina accent penetrated Anton's misery.

He'd liked Katie and his bizarre secret was spooking her off. He didn't think that Isobel would stop Katie's abrupt exit for long.

He should know better than to have hopes. How many friends had he lost because of it? Some thought he was crazy or a liar. But if he hid his remote-viewing ability he'd always slip up somehow. Then they'd think that he really was lying about everything all along, and they'd be gone. The few times he'd tried the truth, he'd been called a "fucking freak." As a general guideline, he tried to avoid getting that response.

His only friends, the only ones he could be himself around, were on the Shadow Force: Psi team. They too had powers they each had to find a way to deal with in the real world.

"It is so very difficult to humble our Michelle," Isobel continued. For a moment, Anton felt some hope.

It also gave him a chance to sneer at his dram-sister, which was always cheering.

"And to place Anton into such frustration without him just barreling through it in his normal style."

Anton sighed when Michelle sneered back at him. He tried to pretend she wasn't right, even though he knew there was no hiding the truth from Isobel. Her gift of empathy was never wrong.

Isobel studied Katie for a long moment, not that she'd ever reveal what she was sensing.

Katie still appeared to be gobsmacked, which almost made Anton smile. Isobel did that to a lot of people. Had done it to him, way back when.

He'd met her when she and Michelle had been college roommates. Even then it was easy to see that she was going to be somebody. He'd never hit on her. Partly because Michelle would have killed him for hitting on her roommate. But also because even back then, Isobel Manella had her shit so together that she was a little scary. He still didn't know quite what to think of her all these years later.

"Don't worry," she addressed Katie. "I can easily see your mix of anger and curiosity without looking any deeper."

Katie didn't say a word.

"A quiet one. Where did Anton find you? He doesn't usually go for the quiet ones."

She was right. Because the quiet ones noticed things; never as fast as Katie just had, but they did. The boisterous and playful women would brush off his occasional off-kilter view of things for far longer. With them he could at least pretend he was having a meaningful relationship…for a while.

Katie glanced at him uncertainly.

"I'm not going for her…for you," he amended when her eyes narrowed. Not that he'd mind. "I just liked watching you watch the badgers."

"You *were* there." She didn't make it a question.

Anton sighed, then nodded. He'd really put his foot in it this time.

"I somehow *knew* you were there. But I didn't see you."

"That's weird." Anton stared down at his beer, not that it helped him think any deeper. Even looking down at the black surface, he couldn't resist a quick glance up with his other vision to watch her honey-amber eyes inspect him with deep suspicion. No one *ever* knew when his vision was lookabout someplace.

"Seriously weird," Katie agreed, definitely still talking about not seeing him rather then sensing him at all. "Care to explain?"

Letting go of his vision, Anton looked over to Isobel for guidance.

She tipped her head slightly in thought, then gently pushed Katie back into her chair before joining them.

Isobel sent Michelle off to fetch her a beer. "Yes, Anton. Why were you watching…"

"Katie," Katie provided when Isobel did one of her single-raised eyebrow things.

"…Katie watch badgers?" She turned back to Katie. "Why were you watching badgers?"

"It's what I do."

"Watch badgers?" Anton tried to imagine that.

"Sounds…fine." He managed to both be insulting and sound like an idiot. Two-for-one the wrong way. Shit!

"I'm a professional wildlife tracker. Now explain how I missed you being there despite Tom Brown Jr.'s training."

Anton noticed Ricardo was suddenly sitting up and paying attention. Isobel hadn't reacted. But Ricardo was a former Delta Force operator and something she'd said had just struck his best friend as very interesting.

"It's because I wasn't physically there," Anton finally admitted when Isobel nodded for him to explain.

When Katie started to protest, he held up his hand to stop her. He'd never set out to prove that he *could* see around corners, usually striving to prove that he couldn't.

"Hold up some number of your fingers behind your back."

When she did, he blurred out of looking at her face, then he stepped his vision around the back of her chair.

Katie had almost followed his motion. No one, not even Isobel could do that.

"Not under your jacket," he told her.

She moved her hand into view from behind, still not visible from anyone's position at the table.

He couldn't help smiling. "My, but that's a rude gesture. Do nice English girls normally give men the bird?" She spun the rest of the way around and looked behind her. Not just behind her, but up at his face.

He let his "vision" go and was looking at her face with his own eyes when she turned back around. "How can you be in two places at once?"

"I can't. But I can be here—and see from there."

"And," Isobel said softly, "You can see him there, which I find utterly fascinating."

Katie shook her head. "No. No, I can't."

But Katie could certainly *feel* him there as clearly as if she could see.

"No! This is too weird."

"Wha'did I miss?" Michelle returned with Isobel's beer. "Damn it. I knew I shouldn't have left."

Two others trailed along behind her. A tall blond man carrying a black cowboy hat and a petite blonde carrying a white one. The woman moved with the grace that Katie recognized as that of a trained tracker.

"Jesse, Hannah...Katie," with a long pause before saying her name. Apparently that was Michelle's idea of a formal introduction.

But she hadn't been here when Katie had introduced herself, had she? She'd hesitated, glanced at Ricardo, then known Katie's name. Was it tattooed on his forehead in invisible ink that only Michelle could see?

Reminding herself to be still and observe was not helping as much as it usually did.

Michelle scooted her chair closer to Ricardo before sitting as the others crowded in. Six was the upper limit of the bowsprit table, especially with the giant sitting beside her. She made seven.

"Evening, ma'am," the cowboy said solemnly. "What's your twist?"

"I don't have a twist," she answered automatically.

"What do you mean *twist?"* And she was afraid that there was a good chance she didn't want to know the answer.

"W'all," his accent matched his Texas hat. "I come in and you're sitting with a bunch of folks as have interesting abilities. I was just a-guessing like you might belong."

"I'm a wildlife tracker. That's all."

"She trained with Tom Brown Jr.," Ricardo said softly.

The petite blonde looked at her sharply. "For real?"

"For real," Katie didn't know what about that so interested Ricardo and Hannah. She'd never met someone who knew about Tom who wasn't a tracker.

"What's the deal with Brown?" Anton asked for her.

Ricardo and Hannah eyed each other, until finally it was Hannah who spoke. "Tom is perhaps the finest tracker alive, if you don't count Colonel Gibson who trained the two of us. Runs a school. That's a serious set of skills if she really pursued it."

"Since I was fourteen," Katie confirmed. Her parents should never have had a child. Boarding school wasn't enough time away, so she'd been shipped to Tom in America each summer like an unwanted parcel.

Isobel hummed thoughtfully, "What did Mr. Brown have to say about your tracking skills?"

Katie tried to see past the dazzle that was Isobel Manella, but it was difficult, as if she was wearing a cloak of herself. Somewhere behind those manslayer-dark eyes and serious curves was an equally serious person. It was almost like seeing-but-not-seeing Anton when he'd supposedly circled behind her.

Isobel smiled to herself as if she knew what Katie was seeing.

"Uncanny," Katie used that single word because, while Tom wasn't much given to speaking about anything other than the trail, he'd remarked on her ability that way several times.

"I'm so surprised." Isobel's tone was a kindly tease. One that Katie didn't understand at all.

"Someone care to explain to this cowboy what in Sam Hill is going on?" Jesse's confusion couldn't be even half of hers.

When Isobel looked at her, Katie just shook her head. She had *no* idea what was happening.

"Remember when you first found your gift?" Isobel asked the others around the table.

Gift? The reactions were fascinating.

Hannah and Jesse actually shuddered. Ricardo and Michelle clasped hands tightly and looked sad. Anton just shrugged. He laughed easily when she turned to face him.

"Like Isobel, I can't remember not knowing. I could always take my vision out for a walk."

"Take your vision. Out for a walk..." Her own voice sounded strained and far away, but she couldn't seem to reel it back in.

He pointed a big finger at the cowboy and Hannah. "They do some mighty strange things with sound. These two are telepathic. Don't worry, only to each other."

Michelle's smile quirked to the side, then Ricardo spoke up, "She says to say, 'Seriously weird, huh?' She's right."

Unable to breathe, Katie turned slowly to look at Isobel.

"I'm an empath. I know what people are feeling. Really feeling rather than just wish they were. Don't worry."

Isobel had said that earlier. And Anton just now. Which was truly *making* her worry.

"I'm not reading you. I keep my gift turned off most of the time. But because it took me a long time to learn to do that, I find facial expressions can be almost as illustrative."

Katie swallowed hard against a dry throat but couldn't seem to lift her beer from the table to slake it. It took her two tries before she could speak.

"Are you saying that I'm…" She had no idea how to finish that sentence.

"A psychometer?" Isobel suggested with a shrug.

"A…what?"

"That's someone who can sense when someone has touched something or been in a place. Added to your tracker training, I suspect that you are better at finding the most elusive animals than almost anyone."

Tom had indeed said something like that.

And she'd just shrugged it off. After four full summers with him, she was practically his co-teacher. Thinking that might have been more than just a trained skill was almost as uncomfortable as having Anton looking over her shoulder…when he wasn't.

She wanted to pound her head on the table to make it feel better. Real.

It didn't take any weirdo gift to know that all it would do is hurt.

CHAPTER 4

Katie didn't feel any better when she woke in the morning.

She normally enjoyed waking. Even after a late night, dawn was the world's softest alarm clock. Her tiny rented flat might not be much bigger than the bed, but it faced east toward the April dawn. She always left the curtains open to welcome the light.

Today she yanked them closed—hard enough to dislodge the rod and it clanked to the floor.

Worse, there wasn't even a single blissful moment before her thoughts were overrun by the fact that she was a bloody freak.

No, it just couldn't be right.

But twenty-twenty hindsight was offering her some awfully relevant memories.

Playing football at boarding school, she always knew when someone was coming up hard from behind to the steal the ball. It had made her a killer center because she could always thread her way through the opposing team without ever losing the ball. She never had to look where her teammates were waiting for the pass, because they were always in the right place.

Or so she'd thought until now.

What if she somehow *knew* where they were and only passed them the ball *when* they were in the right place?

She'd always assumed her childhood hide-and-seek skills were just an early expression of the tracking skills that Tom had always praised.

But what if they weren't?

What if she'd earned the nickname Killjoy Katie through some weirdo "twist" that she'd never asked for?

Were her tracking skills even real? She'd anchored the whole of her self-identity to having and honing those skills. And now she was finding out they weren't hers at all?

She clutched onto the bedsheets to anchor her somewhere in the storm.

There was a knock on her door.

"I'm not a freak!" Katie shouted out at some unsuspecting visitor, then thumped her head back on the pillow.

The silence on the other side of the door was palpable.

"Come in," she called out, but couldn't raise herself to see who had entered.

"It's a problem, isn't it?" Hannah Tucker, the quiet blonde who didn't even stand to the cowboy's shoulder, eased into the room hardly even disturbing the air. She closed the door behind her, which was good. Katie was not at all ready to deal with Isobel, or even worse, Anton. Besides, she was wearing running shorts and an old

"Trackers Do It In The Wild" t-shirt that she loved but had always been too embarrassed to wear in public.

"I'm not a freak," was the only greeting she could think to offer.

Hannah nodded and sat on the foot of the bed. She did it so smoothly that the old mattress didn't even creak.

"How did you learn to do that?"

"Ever hear of the US Army's Delta Force?"

"You? I thought they were like super warriors."

"*We* super warriors come in all sizes."

"And genders." Katie liked that idea.

"I was one of the very few women. But yes."

"And you can…" Katie shrugged. She didn't credit anything she remembered from last night.

Someone snapped their fingers close by her right ear.

Katie twisted, but there was no one there. God help her for even thinking it, she couldn't *sense* anyone having been there either.

"Though for my gift to have any volume, I have to be in contact with Jesse. He acts like an amplifier. I always thought that I was just particularly skilled at the evasion portion of Delta training."

This time there was a crack of a branch in Katie's wardrobe, making her twist to see.

During that momentary distraction, Hannah had risen and moved silently to stand at the window. And, someone save her, Katie had known that even before she'd turned back to see it.

"It takes some getting used to. Are we freaks? We don't know. There are six of us. That's all we know about. Seven now."

"Seven? No! Hold on just a moment." Katie shoved herself upright. "So not! Six! *You,* are *six!*"

Hannah didn't argue. But neither did she conveniently evaporate into thin air along with any memory of her being there to begin with. Instead she picked up the curtain rod and rehung it across the window.

"Six," Katie emphasized.

Hannah simply shrugged. "Why don't you get dressed and we'll go for a walk? It's a beautiful morning. Though still a little cool. You may want a jacket."

Katie tried to find a reason to argue, but nothing came to mind. She gathered up her clothes and went down the hall to the shared bath to clean up and get changed.

Anton hated running. Guys who were six-five were either built for lifting, like him, or they were pencil-necks built for running.

That hadn't stopped Ricardo and Jesse from rousting him before the crack of dawn this morning—midnight in San Antonio. "You have ta get yourself switched on over to the right clock."

He'd rather die peacefully in bed, but they hadn't let that be an option.

His attempts to beg off had only extended the run. They'd started with a stiff climb out of town on Mousehole Lane, *Maw-zel.* He was soon trapped. Ricardo's sense of direction was Delta Force honed. He and Jesse had flown helicopters in the service. Put him up at a fifty meters and clipping along at a couple hundred klicks an hour, and he'd be on it.

Running through these twisting English lanes, at midnight Central Daylight Time, and he knew where he was for about the first thirty seconds. After that he was up shit's creek.

Eventually the sunrise had told him what direction was east for all the good it did him. Somewhere out there lay the town of a mouse's hidey hole—where he *should* be waking up to a lazy breakfast and coffee—but it could now lie north, south, or east. The only reason he knew it wasn't west was because the only thing east of Mousehole was the English Channel.

Anton double-checked, just because his head was so messed up, but he was definitely running, not swimming. So, he wasn't east of Mousehole.

"This is where they must have minted the word bucolic," Jesse offered without the least huff of breathlessness. The big-shouldered cowboy loped along easily beside him.

It was hard not to agree.

Whatever "road" they were on hadn't had a signpost at the turn. Neither one was much more than a paved one-lane track. Close by either side of the pavement ran aged, dry-laid rock walls. Some were shoulder-high, some once had been. They were thick with bramble and birdsong, until suddenly the hedges dropped away. The fields that showed through those gaps ranged from the size of Pa's big, kitchen garden to a space big enough to land a handful of helos.

Some fields were brilliant yellow with rapeseed for

making canola oil. Some were busy with flocks of sheep. Big fluffy beige balls with black faces cropped the grass. Knee-high lambs bounced about like rubber balls on a hard floor.

"Doink-doink-doink!" he called in rhythm to a lamb springing along the other side of the rock wall.

It looked sideways at him in alarm without stopping its forward progress. In moments it was ass over teakettle, then sprinting for its mother with a sharp bleat. It took about three heartbeats for all of the sheep to decide he was "the wolf" and go stampeding off to the far side of the enclosure.

"So much for bucolic," Jesse laughed.

"Dumb as chickens," Anton huffed out as they followed Ricardo back in between more towering hedges.

"Are chickens dumb?"

"Cluck stupid. Only dumber critter on God's green Earth is a turkey; they'll stare up into the sky when its raining as if they can't figure out what in tarnation this wet stuff is. I don't know what old Ben Franklin was thinking about when he wanted them to be the national symbol. Thought you were bread-and-buttered on a farm? How come you don't know that?"

Jesse tipped back his hat. "Daddy runs a ranch, a *Texas* ranch. We have horses."

"They smart?"

"Don't rightly know about that. Not smart like Ricardo and me," Jesse's grin said the tease of leaving out Anton was friendly, so he ignored it…and vowed to get Jesse back later. "Your average horse is actually more smart like Isobel. They know a hundred yards off if you're the afraid-type, intermediate, or an expert horseman. Know how you're feeling long before you do."

"Now you're saying I'm as dumb as a stupid horse?"

"No," Ricardo slowed until they were running three abreast up the road. "Horse knows what he's feeling. Back of the line for you, Anton."

Since that was more words than he usually spoke in a day, Anton responded with, "What are you yabbering on about, Ricardo?"

They reached an intersection. Ricardo led them to the right for no reason Anton could see other than the short steep climb the road made between higher fields. Punishing him for asking? Probably.

"What made you follow Katie to the badgers?"

"I was out in central nowhere, off toward Sennen Cove, just, uh..." he hadn't meant to reveal that. "Just taking a lookabout."

"Just trying to get a one-up on us by pre-scouting the site," Jesse nodded. "Good move. Wish I'd thought of it. 'Course I could point out that Hannah distracted me some yesterday evening so I've got no complaints a'tall. Expect your dram-sister did much the same for Ricardo."

Ricardo's silence confirmed that as he leaned into the hill.

"Must be tough being a single-type person. Why you doing it, pard?"

"Who says I want to settle down any?" Anton managed to gasp out as they neared the hillcrest. "Even if I did, I'm not finding anyone that kind of special crossing my path."

Ricardo just made a disgusted sound and kicked ahead for the top of the rise.

Jesse paced him easily.

Anton dug deep and held his position off their beam… until he cleared the top.

The road turned northwest and inland somewhere. Instead, Ricardo led the way to a path that plunged south down to the sea, then climbed back up the far side of the jagged cove. From their vantage, Anton could see that the path plunged and rose many times between here and the tiny islet in the hazy distance that marked the entrance to Mousehole harbor. At least he hoped it was the same islet or he was so screwed.

CHAPTER 5

Katie grabbed her normal sausage-and-fried-egg bap and to-go coffee from the Four Teas Cafe.

Hannah didn't say a word as she led them to a bench along at the north tip of the small harbor. To the right was the sweep of Grenfell Street past the market and Ship Inn, before it ducked back into the granite buildings that made up the waterfront and the wharf. To their left, the big seawall arced in from either side. As it was a busy April weekend, the wall tops were packed with their limit of about twenty cars apiece.

Low tide. The harbor itself, seventy-five meters wide and twice that long, was damp sand and flat rock except for close by the gap in the seawall. Fifty-odd pleasure and fishing boats dotted the exposed seabed and waited for the four-meter tide to refloat them. Any working fisherman would have left on the midnight high tide.

They sat quietly while Katie ate her breakfast. Hannah appeared to simply be enjoying the morning sun shining off the sea. It was the most relaxed Katie had been…in a long while.

When *had* she last stopped? Making a go of her tracking business didn't exactly rain down the money. The BBC *Springwatch* had been nice.

For weeks every year, the BBC set up cameras and recorded the local birds, mammals, even fish. She'd helped them scout the area and embed their cameras. Some were easy, along a badger trail or in a stoat den. Some tricky, inside a flicker's nest or monitoring a caterpillar's cocoon.

But that was over. *Autumnwatch* was months off, and other than odd jobs like the charming Chas Thorstad, she wasn't exactly thriving. Wouldn't even be much afloat doing that without Anton. She had plenty of family money, but she'd cut off an arm before she'd touch the account her parents dumped more money into whenever they felt guilty about how they'd raised their only daughter.

While she still didn't know how she felt about Anton, she appreciated him stepping in to shake down Chas. She'd needed that fee. And Anton hadn't applied any payback pressure afterward. Most guys would have acted as if they'd suddenly been entitled to take her to bed. But Anton had done the exact opposite, scooting away to his friends like a very, very tall spooked puppy dog.

Had he really just cared about justice?

Maybe so.

Was it before or after he shook down Chas that he'd recognized her—if that's what he'd done?

After. He tossed Chas out the door, turned to her, then sworn to her face in surprise.

No way to fake that reaction.

So, check the box that inside the mountain of a man was a decent guy. A fact that seemed to be confirmed by the quality of his friends.

But the only way Anton could he have seen her was if he was in on some scam with Chas. Yet he'd thrown Chas through the door like a rag doll, so that wasn't the answer either.

That must mean that he *could* do what he said he could. Which made even less sense. Weird magical psi powers were fairy tales, not real world.

And that same cycle of logic leading nowhere had cost her most of a night's sleep with no brilliant insights.

She'd learned long ago about living in the real world. Her parents had made sure of that. They'd as good as thrown her away. And Tom had taught her that the only thing that mattered was detailed observation of the world around her.

No. She wasn't some mythic freak who…

Katie almost didn't hear her when Hannah finally spoke. Had almost forgotten she was there beside her on the bench because she'd gone so quiet.

"I was just thinking about Isobel…" And Hannah's voice trailed away.

Isobel. Of course, a Hollywood type would be into magic and crystals and whatnot. Except Isobel seemed more grounded in reality than any other person Katie had ever met.

They'd chatted briefly about places in town that Isobel had explored yesterday evening before they'd met in the

Ship Inn's pub. Katie had made some suggestions of cute things that Isobel might have missed.

The glass porthole in the side of Cregyn Cottage that showed the entrance to an old smugglers' tunnel used by 18th century tobacco runners trying to avoid the revenue man.

The most recent yarn-bombing, a line of knit cats prowling along a second-story balcony. In the early 2010s, the Graffiti Grannies had yarn-bombed many places in town, most in the cat-mouse theme. Katie rather hoped this was a rebirth. It was enough to make her take up knitting again.

Katie could easily imagine Isobel wandering out of Ship Inn south to Cregyn. Then winding back along Mill Pool and North Street to see the cats and one of Katie's favorite gardens. Finally wandering down Commercial Road and up Parade Hill to come back to the harbor along the north leg of the South West Coast Trail, which led up right behind their bench.

Katie glanced back, then would have fallen off the bench if Hannah hadn't grabbed her arm.

"How long have you been there?" But she could see that Isobel was just walking up to them…from exactly the direction Katie had just been daydreaming.

Daydreaming?

"She's got it," Hannah said to Isobel.

"Got what? The hiccups? You spooked the crap out of me. They're so far gone that they're never coming back now. And dammit, I liked my hiccups."

Isobel smiled at the joke, then circled around to sit on Hannah's other side. "But I wouldn't have spooked you if you'd just accepted that I'd be where you already knew I was."

"Not happening. So not happening." Katie turned to stare back out at the small harbor.

Even as she watched, three men came into view where the South West Coast Trail disappeared beyond the harbor.

"Is that them?" She was sorry she'd spoken. But the trio had broken the pattern of motion drawing her eye. And once she'd spotted them, there was no question who they were. At least that was her tracking skill of noticing details and not...whatever these women were talking about.

The three men started to run along the street, but then the smallest of the trio turned sharply. The other two followed and they ran down the boat ramp. In moments they were racing across the sand and rock toward their bench.

The smallest of the three, Ricardo, ran as if he was floating along, barely in contact with anything so mundane as the ground. There was a perfect conservation of movement.

"How did they know we were here?" Because they were making a straight beeline toward their bench as they raced across the dry harbor.

"Oh, I told my man. Isn't he just so pretty?" Michelle had come up behind them.

Then Katie realized that Michelle had probably told him using telepathy, which would explain their abrupt course change.

It also made Katie feel a little nauseous.

Hannah's agreeing sigh was all for the tall blond man, wearing his black cowboy hat even on a run.

And using his massive power and long legs to advantage, Anton overtook them and came first to the harbor's north stairs. He sprinted to the top, three steps at a time.

At the very top, he halted and grabbed both railings, clearly set to let the others bounce off his back.

Then he spotted her.

"Katie!"

He let go his grip and made it half a step before the other two reached the head of the stairs and flattened him against the railing.

Anton had kind of assumed that Katie would be gone. Or at least wouldn't want anything to do with them. Or him.

After revealing what they were—and her insisting what she wasn't—she'd left as soon as British politeness allowed.

Yet here she was.

And here he was, nearly blasted over the steel railing and back down into the harbor below. The top rail, chest high on most folks, had caught him square in the solar plexus.

He'd already been out of wind before he'd decided it was time to outrun Ricardo and Jesse. He still wasn't sure how, but he'd done it.

And now he had no air at all and let himself simply

slide down to his knees and wheeze like a helo turboshaft engine robbed of fuel.

"That was great!" Katie was helping him ease into a sitting position on the sidewalk with his back against the traitorous railing. "How far did you run?"

Anton flapped a hand in Ricardo's direction.

"Nothing much. Just a 10K."

Anton glared at him. The man was sweating, but he didn't look tapped at all. At least Jesse had the decency to look hammered.

"Maybe fifteen," Ricardo's evil smile said it might have been twenty.

Anton made wavy motions with his hand for Katie, because he still didn't have the air to speak, only getting tiny gulps past the pain in his chest. Not the sort of manly man moment he'd like Katie to be witnessing.

"Up and down the hills of Cornwall," she understood right away. "Be glad you weren't in northern Cornwall. Brown Willy is four hundred meters."

"Brown Willy?" He managed to grunt out in surprise. A willy was British slang for a man's—

Katie rolled her eyes at his tone. "That's the name of the highest point in the county, not a pickup line for a big black man. It comes from the Cornish *Bronn Ewhella,* meaning highest hill."

"Damn, and I had such hopes." He went for a joke to cover up any awkwardness. And that's when Anton finally figured out what Ricardo was talking about. He actually *did* have some hopes.

"This isn't the Stone Age."

"No, but—" he managed before he ran out of air again.

“This is England,” Katie continued. “Not the backward puritanical hole that sits across the pond. Here you’re just another bloke. Sorry if you find that disappointing.”

He couldn’t help but smile at her. She would be… already was an easy woman to get to like.

He also liked that Katie wasn’t a screen beauty like Isobel, or the in-your-face kind like his stepsister. She was like Hannah; just so completely herself. No bullshit show or teasing displays.

Katie had a quiet steadiness that pervaded her being even when she was upset. And instead of gorgeous, she wore pretty with an ease few women could pull off with absolutely no affectation. She wore comfortable shorts and a blouse that had seen some hard wear, but was quality material so it still looked good. Practical sneakers had replaced the soft leather moccasins she’d been wearing last night.

“What was with the moccasins?”

“That’s what you ask me after comparing your privates to a mountain?” Katie looked at him askance.

“Well, first, I don’t see how four hundred meters makes a mountain as long as I don’t have to run up it. And second…yeah, I guess it is.”

She rose and helped him to his feet. “Moccasins leave less impression on the ground. They let me feel a twig before I snap it, and I have better control for balance. Unless I’m tracking on very rough terrain, it’s what I wear.”

Anton nodded. It was interesting, but she was right: it was the wrong question.

“You’re still here?” That was the right one.

Until he saw her face.

Maybe not so much.

"Do you want to talk about it?"

She shook her head in a flurry of hair that she then had to scoop back over her shoulder.

He wanted to reach out and brush it back into place, but resisted.

Then she shrugged as if maybe she should talk about it even if she didn't want to.

He was about to lead her toward the long pier of the northern half of the seawall when Isobel raised her voice.

"You have twenty minutes to clean up and grab breakfast, boys. Then we're on the move."

Crap! No way to duck out. They hadn't been sent to England as a vacation. But now he'd risk losing track of Katie again and he didn't like that idea at all.

"Where are you all going?"

Isobel just smiled at Katie. "You'll see."

CHAPTER 6

Anton had picked up Katie's trail just *here* last night.

Land's End Airport lay behind them. The heat signature of her footsteps had faded, then been erased by the morning sunlight, but he could walk the path blindfolded. Could still picture her lying prone at the edge of the wood in front of the badger holes. The fine promise of the exceptional view from behind had definitely delivered on the woman from the front.

"What was that guy photographing?"

"What guy?" Jesse asked him.

"The one I tossed through the pub door."

"Dang. I missed that?" Then like the sap the cowboy was, he grinned at Hannah. "Still totally worth it," making very clear exactly what they'd been doing before coming down for a drink last night.

And despite being Delta Force-trained like Ricardo, Hannah returned his mushy smile.

"Are they always like that?" Katie whispered to him.

"Hard to say. Definitely since the day we met them. But they'd been together a while by then. Like twenty-four hours anyway."

She smiled along with his low chuckle.

"Forty-eight," Hannah corrected. "And we weren't like that…this…that fast."

"Forty-two hours and twenty minutes," Jesse added. "And I was already as gone on Hannah as a steak on a hot grill by then."

"You see why I keep him?" Hannah asked Katie matter-of-factly before tapping her matching white cowboy hat up by the brim and pulling Jesse down for a steamy kiss.

Michelle made some pithy comment that Anton didn't quite catch because he was suddenly picturing what it might be like to kiss Katie Whitfield. That thought hadn't really crossed his mind before this moment and he liked that thought…a lot.

"Chas," Katie cleared her throat but gave him no clue what she was thinking, "was photographing an erythristic badger. It's a very rare coloring mutation that makes it red-and-white rather than black-and-white."

"No. I mean I saw that cute little guy. But that's not what he was photographing."

Katie opened her mouth with a question when Isobel doubled back to the place the four of them had stopped.

"Somewhere here is the assignment. Our challenge is to find it and infiltrate the installation to test their security."

"Here?" Anton looked around.

They stood halfway between the airport and a long

beach that stretched a kilometer south to a small hamlet. Between the two was all sheep pastures and rock walls dotted with quaint farmhouses.

"Aren't we being a little obvious tramping across their property?"

It was Katie who shook her head in response, "Ever hear of The Ramblers?"

Anton shrugged a no.

She smiled up at him. "Anton, you just haven't lived in the right places. All of the UK is a network of walking trails. A few are broad and paved, but most are little more than this track we've been on."

Below the airport, there was the copse of trees where he'd found Katie and Chas last night off to their right. A kilometer ahead lay a long beach and the sea caught between a pair of rocky headlands.

From where they stood down to the beach and all along to the south lay a patchwork of fields crisscrossed by stone walls. Anton had assumed they were on a sheep path in one of those fields, but now he noticed that it crossed through field after field in a roughly straight line. There were gates he hadn't noticed where the track crossed fence lines.

"By ancient law, these paths belong to the people, not the landowners. Some of them cut through the heart of major estates. There are many American rock and roll stars who tried to buy luxury estates here, only to discover that, by law, their adoring fans could walk through their property, sometimes within ten meters of the back door because that's where an old trail lay. Right now, as far as anyone else is concerned, we're just a group of ramblers out for a tramp."

Anton looked. The men were a scruffy lot. Jeans and t-shirts for the most part. Hannah was dressed much the same. Michelle had been a fashion gal before she became a paramedic and then fell in love with Ricardo, and it showed. Slacks, a flowered blouse, and a cheery sunhat. Isobel wore a happy sundress that made her look like poured gold.

Katie was dressed in the same clothes as yesterday. A nice blouse and jeans that looked wonderfully real.

"Okay, so we're ramblers."

"Uh-huh," then Katie turned to inspect the fields herself. "So what are we looking for?"

"You know those undersea cable things?" Anton couldn't resist the tease.

"Yes..." she agreed carefully.

"We're looking for those."

Katie studied him as if he'd lost his mind.

He couldn't help grinning down at her.

"But we're on land," Katie said it carefully.

She could almost half believe that these people had some sort of powers, though she didn't know when part of her thinking had changed. Phrases like "helicopter pilots" and "former Delta Force" had passed by without her really connecting the pieces.

There was a lot of US Military in this group.

Which gave her no clue to what they were actually doing in her country.

"Who are you people?"

Michelle slipped an arm through hers like they were lifetime girlfriends. "We call ourselves Shadow Force: Psi. Psi like in special parapsychological abilities. We're… uh…" Words seemed to fail Michelle at that point which, by Isobel's smile, was a very uncommon occurrence.

"Think of us as specialized troubleshooters," Isobel explained easily. "And what we're interested in this morning is where the undersea cables come to land."

"That's easy," Katie pointed down toward the beach. "Just read the signs facing the sea that say, 'Don't anchor here'."

There was a brief silence, then Anton snorted with laughter. "Okay, who else missed that one?"

There were many chagrined looks.

"Not a sailor in the lot of them," Isobel remarked dryly. "I learned about those signs when I was filming *Where Dreams Sail.*"

It was like a snap of Hannah's disembodied fingers just in front of Katie's nose. For a moment she'd forgotten who Isobel Manella was in *real* life. It had been a lovely romantic comedy set in and around Seattle, Washington. Katie remembered the pretty fifty-foot sailboat that had been the hero's home. And a steamy sex scene aboard… that suddenly had Katie struggling not to blush.

Again, Isobel's understanding smile. Somehow, she brought all of her credibility to the team and made everything they were claiming seem almost possible.

Isobel was kind enough to change the subject. "It's easy

enough to see roughly where they come ashore, though they're well buried. But where do they go from there is our first challenge. There are seven undersea cables that come ashore along Sennen Cove. Four local cables come in from Ireland, France, and the Scilly Islands. Two more come across from the Americas. And the twenty-eight-thousand-kilometer FLAG Europe-Asia that connects eighteen countries from here through the Mediterranean, Suez, Indian Ocean, and up to China, Korea, and Japan. That's the one we were tasked with testing the security on. The first step is finding it."

Katie pointed off to the southeast. "Actually, FEA and FLAG-1, which reaches to New York, both come ashore at PK, that's Porthcurno, about halfway back to Mousehole."

They all blinked at her in surprise, close enough in unison to make her laugh. Something she hadn't done in a long while.

"Shit!" Ricardo recovered first. "We ran through there this morning."

"We did?" Anton swiveled his head around as if he could see it from here and ended up looking in completely in the wrong direction.

He finally groaned and turned back to her.

"I have no sense of direction here. From my family's farm in North Carolina, the sea does a fine job staying to the east. From San Antonio, the Gulf of Mexico is always to the south."

"Southeast," Michelle cut in.

"Hush when your betters are talking."

Anton ignored the fist that thudded against his back,

aside from winking at Katie.

"Here it's just all messed up with the sea on every which side. Can't seem to get a hold on it. Anyway, our colonel has a weird sense of humor. It's probably his idea of a rip-roaring joke to tell us to start off with Sennen Cove and see what we find. How did you know about the FEA cable anyway? Are you a plant by Colonel Gibson?"

Katie shrugged. "All the locals know. It was cut into Porthcurno when I was a kid in 2001. There are so many cables that come ashore in Cornwall that the locals keep a tally like a game. Porthcurno received the two FLAG cables—short for Fiber-optic Link Around the Globe—for the US and Asia links. But Bude up north is getting the new 2Africa cable."

She saw Isobel and Michelle exchange quick glances. A moment later, Ricardo swiveled around to stare at Michelle, then her. Katie sighed, exactly as if Michelle had spoken to him without making a sound.

Anton leaned down to whisper loudly by Katie's ear. "Don'tcha just hate it when they do that mind-to-mind thing?"

"Is Isobel telepathic, too?" It was hard to believe those words had just come out of her mouth.

"Nah. But she and Michelle were college roommates for four years. They developed some weird secret women's language ever since then. Well, if the cable comes up somewhere else, I guess that we'd better go there. Then we can trace where it goes."

Katie again couldn't help laughing, just because she knew it would irritate Anton. It worked.

"What now?" He let out a long-suffering sigh.

"If we trundle back to Mousehole by way of Porthcurno, we'll drive close by the main junction point for all of the southern Cornwall cables. It's halfway between these cables and Porthcurno. It's named Skewjack. Skewjack Farms used to be a big hippie, surfing enclave back in the day. All the locals know about this area."

CHAPTER 7

Anton had almost thought Katie was pulling their leg. For one thing, he'd never met a woman who laughed so easily. For another, one who lit up so much each time she did.

But, exactly as she'd said, just five kilometers from Land's End Airport, they drove by it. Skewjack was a low, rounded building, like a Quonset hut on steroids that someone had flattened until it was little more than a massive metal hump. There were only glimpses through a perimeter of trees, but if she was giving it to them straight, it was right there for all to see.

"Take a left here," Katie pointed out an even narrower road than the "main" A30 that they were on.

"We don't want to be too obvious."

"It won't be. There are a couple farms back there. If Janice is in, we can go visit Bunker Cottage. This whole area is an old RAF radar site. She converted one of their bunkers into a lovely little tourist place."

Hannah steered them in. The screen of trees wrapped

around the second side of the Skewjack building, but thinned along the third.

Anton tried to appear casual as he studied it out the window. To the back was a row of massive air conditioning units and big emergency generators. If a dozen undersea cables all terminated here, they'd need massive computing power, which would generate a lot of heat.

There were only three cars in the parking lot at the other end. And it was all wrapped in a three-meter-high fence topped with razor wire. The building was studded with security cameras.

Katie definitely wasn't pulling their leg.

The final key was that there were no signs identifying the building. The main gate's only label said to keep out.

Hannah drove them another three hundred meters and pulled over where Katie indicated. They were in the middle of cultivated fields. One was a big sheep paddock, but two were row crops, and the fourth looked like an orchard of hazelnut trees or something.

Bunker Cottage, now that they could see it, had absolutely been a bunker. In the middle of the flat landscape, a grassy earth mound rose from the north. Then partway along, it was chopped off and a wall of mostly windows had been installed. In front of the bunker's opening, a sitting area of wooden chairs and a slightly wild English garden made it look very cozy. Though he'd never pictured scattered palm trees in an English garden, they seemed to fit.

As the others got out of the car, Anton knew what he needed to do. "I'll just stay in the car."

Katie hesitated halfway out the door, then looked back at him. "You're going to…" He could see her swallow hard.

He nodded. Now was where she dismissed him as a freak. And this time he wasn't going to be able to just shrug it off when she did. He liked her.

"Really?"

He sighed. "How many fingers are you holding up behind your back?" This time both her hands were in plain view, but she caught the reference to last night's demonstration.

She stared down at the car's floor for a long moment. When she finally spoke, it was so softly that he could barely hear her.

"And you think that I…can do…something that…"

"Something strange and kind of cool that's scaring the crap out of you?"

Katie just nodded, looking up at him through where her hair had fallen forward again. This time he didn't resist the urge to brush it back so that he could see the honey-amber color of her eyes.

"Yeah, Katie. I'm guessing you do. It'll be okay."

"Can you prove it?" But her tone was wry.

"Sure. Later. Maybe over dinner…without those jokers horning in."

"I think I'd like that." And they traded smiles.

Was it a date? Stupid question. Woman was freaking and it was his job to calm her down some.

"But right now I need to go take a hike."

"Isn't that my line?" She didn't wait for his answer. "A hike while sitting in a car?"

"While sitting in a car."

She studied him a moment longer, then nodded before following the others toward Bunker Cottage.

Anton closed his eyes and let his vision slip out after her.

Katie walked like Ricardo and Hannah, as if she wasn't quite touching the ground. Only she did it better. When a woman was better than a pair of Delta Force operators, that was a hell of a sight to see.

She turned to look at him. Not where he sat in the car. Him. Watching her.

Damn! Couldn't get away with shit with this woman.

He headed back up the lane toward Skewjack.

After Anton had declared he was done peeking around Skewjack, they'd all driven the few kilometers south to Porthcurno—the tiny town where so many undersea cables surfaced.

Katie had played tour guide as they'd strolled all through town, all two blocks and a beach of it, before climbing up to the top of the cliff that rose fifty meters above the sea.

Anton's whisper tickled her ear, "Too bad you aren't a TK. We could really use a TK for this."

"TK?" The words slipped out before Katie could stop them. "We're in PK…"

"Why's Porthcurno called that anyway? Mousehole isn't MH. And shouldn't it be PC?"

Katie waved a hand and Anton and the others looked around. They were seated in one of her favorite spots on the Cornish coast. The tiny village was slipped into a sharp, narrow valley. The only road in and out was appropriately named "The Valley." The short sandy beach lay just to the east. But here, atop a jagged cliff just south of the beach, sat the Minack Theatre.

Carved from the granite by an eccentric woman in the 1920s and '30s, the outdoor amphitheater boasted a circular stage, backed by a partial stone wall and a vertical drop to the sea. The broad steps of the curved seating would have fit perfectly in an old Greek theater. Shakespeare under the stars were her favorite performances. She could feel—

Bloody hell!

She *could* feel the actors who had stridden across this stage time and again only to—

Katie shut out the thought and covered it over with more explanations.

"Many of the early transatlantic cables were landed here. By the Second World War, this was the largest undersea cable hub in the world. During the war, they dug deep tunnels under this very cliff to protect the cables and their operators. Telegraphy was all done in Morse code, and PK was Porthcurno's call sign. In Cornish, curno is spelled with a K and it means Pinnacle Cove."

"Oh," Anton looked around again. "Not what we need. We need a telekinetic, with a *T*, to go in and knock out Skewjack's cameras and unlock the gate so that we can get in without them seeing us."

"Isn't that cheating? I mean if the security is good enough to stop people who are normal, isn't that—" Her voice actually squeaked as she cut herself off in panic.

Anton's big hand rested over hers and held on until she could start to breathe again.

"Sorry, I—"

"No skin off any of our backs, Katie. It's okay. We all have lived with it long enough to know that we're more than a little outside the curve."

She clenched his hand in both of hers when he went to let go. She didn't care what other people thought, he simply made her feel better.

The only people seated in the theater at the moment were Anton's team, and she could certainly see that they were thinking about something happy. Michelle took Ricardo's hand and Jesse took Hannah's, and Isobel just offered one of her beautiful smiles.

Katie thought better of it and let go of Anton's hand.

CHAPTER 8

Cornwall was having a typical April evening, surprisingly chilly after the warmth of the day. At least the sea fog was staying just offshore.

Katie lay beside Anton atop the hump of Bunker Cottage, which offered a splendid view of the Skewjack building, especially with the powerful night-vision binoculars that the team had provided.

The team. Michelle, Isobel, and Jesse lay with them. Ricardo and Hannah were somewhere out there in the night.

Again she wondered if she was doing something horribly wrong. Perhaps she should have reported them all to the police or the telephone company. Maybe to the social media sites that owned so many of the cables. Or someone.

These people were invading a site that they themselves had told her was of critical national security. Critical to nations at both ends of the cables, and now she was complicit with helping them attack the UK's terminus.

If that's what they were doing.

She'd looked it up. Not counting all of the little cables to Ireland and Europe, almost every major cable came up in Cornwall or Somerset. It was a little unnerving to realize that three small bombs could essentially sever the UK from the rest of the world. Internet, phones, financial data, all of it. Of course the financial data wasn't such a big concern considering her current bank balance.

Was Isobel Manella a sham? Some sort of secret agent?

Well, actually, she'd said they all were, but for the US government.

They didn't feel bad.

Feel! There was that stupid word again. She just…

Deep breath, Katie. Deep breath.

One of the things she could feel so easily was Anton lying beside her. Except he wasn't using binoculars. He was stretched out on his back, *not* staring at the stars. Somehow, his mind was inside the Skewjack building.

But his body was here, as he proved by reaching out and taking her hand. It was so much bigger than hers that it should feel strange and awkward. Instead, it felt safe, as if he could hold back the world with hands like those.

"Inbound," Jesse said softly.

Katie looked toward Skewjack.

The next technician's shift was coming in. Two cars rolled up to the front gate. The gate opened almost immediately.

Anton spoke up, "Tell them to follow the second car for three meters past the gate, then roll off to the left."

Michelle was silent, apparently relaying the message telepathically to Ricardo.

When she'd asked why they didn't just use radios, Ricardo had explained that they might have systems to monitor that, but that no one had a way to pick up on their telepathy.

Even watching for them, she could barely see Ricardo and Hannah slipping through Skewjack's front gate behind the second car. Dressed in black and carrying no weapons, they moved as smoothly as the shadows they were hiding in.

No weapons. She'd take that as a good sign that this really was just a test.

"Oh come on, guys. You're making this too easy," Anton groaned. Then he spoke quickly, "The staff are inside jawing it up. Nobody looking at the security monitors. Approach from the left corner at sixty degrees. That'll keep you clear of the cameras, just in case someone turns around. Move. Move. Move."

Katie couldn't spot the two former Delta Force operators this time until they were actually at the front door.

Hannah crouched and quickly picked the lock and opened the door.

"Clear to go through. Cut hard right across the threshold."

"In and holding," Michelle spoke for the first time, apparently repeating something Ricardo had told her. From inside the building over a hundred meters away. Without a phone or radio.

Katie buried her face in the thick grass.

"Call this number," then Anton called it out.

"How did you..."

"Reading it off the face of their own desk phone. Call it now, Isobel!"

For some reason, that simple act was what really brought it home for her. He and the others *were* inside that building, reading a secure phone number.

"Ringing," Michelle and Isobel said almost simultaneously. One reporting from Ricardo, and one with the phone to her ear.

"Hello," Isobel spoke up in a calm and pleasant voice when it was answered. "I hope you're having a wonderful evening… You are? Good. Now I'd like you to remain very calm. There's no threat. But your site has been the subject of a security test… No, this isn't a hoax. We've placed two people inside your building. They're unarmed and no threat to you. We just didn't want to surprise you unduly."

"She is so smooth," Katie whispered to Anton.

"Hello. Professional actress. Though she had her shit together even back in college enough to humble any man." He kept his voice soft enough that they could have been alone under the stars.

"Is that the real reason why you never went for Isobel?"

"No, it's because she's scary."

Katie narrowed her eyes at him. She'd already learned that he was a pushover and that was all the push it took.

Then she remembered that he couldn't see her between the darkness and his vision being inside the building. Just as she started feeling foolish, Anton shrugged.

"She was Michelle's roommate and best friend.

Michelle needed a friend really badly at that point in her life. I didn't want to mess that up."

How could such a big man be so sweet?

"There was never any real click anyway." He squeezed her hand, indicating he felt one with her. It gave her stomach a quick flip of vertigo, like when she'd watched guillemot chicks leap from the cliff before they could really fly.

He was here.

And there.

And she was still holding his hand for reasons that were thoroughly perplexing. She'd never really been the handholding type. It implied trust, something that her parents and the boarding school had taught her to never have.

Trust nothing and no one.

Tom Brown Jr. suffered from a similar affliction, he just assumed that anyone who wasn't himself wasn't quite good enough. Even when she did something perfectly, that she was pretty sure he couldn't have duplicated, he'd find something to pick apart as if dissecting a specimen for study. Maybe just trying to make her even better, but it had still stung.

"What are they doing?" Isobel asked softly. "They're reluctant to believe me."

Anton hesitated just a moment. "Woman on the phone is looking bored. Other three are still jawing. Carrot top is scratching his balls."

Isobel spoke into her phone again. "Why don't you put me on speaker phone? Or at least tell your red-headed teammate that it isn't polite to scratch his genitals in the presence of a woman."

"That got a response," Michelle reported from Ricardo.

"Yeah," Anton laughed. "She's staring at the ceiling looking for a hidden camera."

"She also yelled at Andrew to stop it and check the area." Ricardo-through-Michelle again.

"Is Andrew always so thoughtless?" Isobel asked ever so politely. "I'd say that's enough of a test. My people are going to stand up now, introduce themselves, and then we'll leave. The report will be filed with no criticism of yourselves as your jobs are to be technicians, not security officers. There are clearly some large problems with that side of the operation."

Anton laughed aloud.

"What?"

"Hannah just stepped out of the shadows to join the circle of three guys as if she'd always been there. Ricardo sat in the chair across the desk from the woman on the phone before she even saw him. The four are twitching worse than a hound dog dreaming of a thousand rabbits."

Anton was strolling back toward the rest of the team with Ricardo and Hannah. He didn't know why. They were Delta Force, so it wasn't as if he would hear anything or see anything new. He just liked the idea of walking idly toward Katie where he could still feel her holding his hand.

Just outside the gate, opened and closed by a very

watchful team leader, they were less than halfway back when Katie's grip tightened hard.

"Hold it."

"What?" He popped back into his body and turned to look at her.

"No. Go back. I've lost it now."

Because he'd just left the spot outside Skewjack's gates, he was able to slip out there again. The fast back-and-forth volley left him feeling a little nauseous, but he did it.

"There!" Katie practically shouted in his ear.

"Easy, girl. What's going on?"

"Walk back and forth a bit."

Anton looked around. Ricardo and Hannah had kept walking, never noticing his departure or return. But now Ricardo stopped and signaled Hannah to do the same. Michelle must have passed on that something was going screwy.

Anton retraced his steps toward Skewjack's gates. When Katie didn't say anything, he walked over to join Ricardo and Hannah who were scanning widely for possible threats.

"Off to…" Katie sounded as if she was grinding her teeth. "I don't know. I can't see anything. But I can feel it."

"What?"

"How the hell should I know?"

Anton tried to picture what was happening. Katie was somehow feeling things through his wandering vision. She might doubt her own abilities, but he didn't.

"Okay, let's try a game."

"A what?" Her voice would have been shrill if not for

that lovely English accent of hers that made everything sound so charming.

"Warmer-cooler. You know that one? Tell me if I'm getting warmer or cooler on whatever it is you're feeling."

"That's nuts."

Anton wasn't going to argue the point.

He strolled across the road to the west, and heard a groan before Katie mumbled out, "Cooler."

He turned and walked back the other way, past Ricardo and Hannah who were still on alert but didn't react at all to his passage, and stepped through the low stone wall.

"This can't be happening! Warmer!"

She jerked her hand out of his. He missed it right away. Could feel the chill night air replace her warm grasp. They were good, strong hands. It was easy to tell that she didn't push papers for a living.

"Wait. Now I can't feel anything. Maybe I was making it all up."

There was a long pause, then she tentatively put her hand on his arm. "Ruddy hell! Warmer!"

He kept going out into the pasture. "So there's something about our physical contact that let's you feel wherever I'm seeing."

Somewhere in the background he could hear Michelle explaining it to the others.

"Wait. Go back a step. Now go side to side. I guess, whatever. I don't know where you are."

Playing warmer-cooler led him behind a clump of five or six small trees. Wire mesh had been wrapped around each trunk to stop the pasture's sheep from chewing them down.

"Right here," Anton turned to Ricardo and pointed at the ground.

Ricardo didn't move his mouth, but moments later he could hear Michelle repeat his telepathic words, with her own interpretation, of course.

"Right where, you big ox? He can't see you."

"Oh sorry. Twenty paces toward the water from where he's standing."

Then Michelle spoke up, "There's water in every direction from here, you dingus."

Katie giggled, she actually giggled, which had been the whole point. He wanted to see how that lit up her face, but he didn't want to lose his place either.

He described his location to Michelle. In moments, Ricardo and Hannah were on the move. It was actually fascinating to watch them move in on the point. They followed no direct line, actually swinging wide and quartering the area.

"Tell them there's no one here now."

The only change they made to their routine was Ricardo nodding his head when Michelle passed on the information.

He had to step aside so that they didn't walk through him—which he wouldn't feel but was still weird—as they finally both arrived at the same spot from different directions.

Ricardo turned and looked toward Skewjack.

Anton followed his line of sight. If someone had lain

here, they were in a perfect position to observe everything about the compound.

"Any idea who it was?" Anton asked Ricardo, forgetting for the moment that Ricardo couldn't hear him.

Michelle was damned efficient as Ricardo shook his head just moments later. A Delta operator wouldn't forget something as simple as Anton not being able to hear him.

But Katie made an uncomfortable sound.

"What?"

When she didn't answer, he let go of his vision and slid once more behind his own eyes.

"Do *you* know who it was?"

"It felt like…" She buried her head against his shoulder. Her hair was even softer than he'd imagined as she mumbled against him. "I can't believe I'm going to say this. It's like I'm selling my soul to Satan or something. It felt like…that guy you threw out of the pub."

"Chas Thorstad?"

She nodded silently.

"Hang on." He couldn't send himself back to where the badgers had been last night. Over thirty hours was far too long ago.

But under twelve hours ago he'd been standing with Katie when they'd all trooped past where he'd picked up her trail behind Land's End Airport.

That was far too long as well.

But even as he had the thought, he was back to the exact spot where Katie had first taken his hand while standing along that trail.

Maybe Katie's presence beside him at that time had made the place sort of bookmarked?

He'd worry about how later.

He ran toward where the badgers had been—thankfully it wasn't far, because it was like swimming through mud by the time he arrived. He stopped where he'd first seen Katie's fine figure stretched out on the ground. Damn but she was a looker from every angle—the lovely English lass of cliché and song.

She wasn't here now and he didn't bother looking at the badgers roaming freely over the hillside with no one around to disturb them.

Instead he sat where Chas Thorstad had been.

Then he turned in the direction that the man's big camera lens had been pointed. Out of sight behind Katie's back. It certainly hadn't been at the badgers.

He spoke aloud to Katie. "About a hundred meters from the badgers. Toward the damned water. What's the white building off by itself? Without a barn."

"You're not here, are you? This is going to make me crazy. Where are you? Oh the badgers? Sennen Cove? Of course you are. Looks like a slightly rundown farmhouse but with no cars or anything else you'd expect?" Katie was also smart as a whip.

"That's the one."

"It would be the terminus building for the Sennen Cove cables. They land there and then jump to land cables which are routed here to Skewjack. Why?"

Anton let go the vision and sat up just as Ricardo and Hannah rejoined their group on the grass atop Bunker Cottage.

"We got a problem, folks. This jerkwad who tried to stiff Katie for her scouting fee was using her to get close to the Sennen Cove cable landing points with a damned big camera. And he was here checking out Skewjack. It's a good bet that he hit Porthcurno as well."

He didn't need to have served ten years in the Army to know how suspicious that was. Neither did anyone else.

Katie was the first to speak. "The only major cable site he's missed in Cornwall would be Widemouth Bay near Bude. That's two hours north of here."

"We can be there before dawn," Hannah turned to walk down the grassy back of Bunker Cottage, heading toward the SUV as if everything was decided.

"Let's go." Anton pushed to his feet and held out a hand to help Katie up.

"No. I have a client tomorrow. I need sleep. I need—"

"Cancel 'em. Sleep later."

"No, Anton. I need the job. I need the money."

"There are three problems with that, Katie," Anton took both of her hands and pulled her to her feet. They ended up standing so close together that he was tempted to continue the motion and just toss her over his shoulder to cart her away. He suspected that wouldn't go over especially well.

"What?"

"First, you're making far more money working with Shadow Force: Psi. The US government doesn't stint when it comes to specialty contractors."

"I don't work for you."

"Not yet. But you work *with* us, and in my book, we're paying you."

"But—"

"Number Two," he turned her to face Skewjack just as

four very official-looking vehicles raced up to the gate. Well-armed soldiers in camouflage uniforms poured out of the doors. "Unless you want to spend your next couple days trying to explain us to them, I'm thinking you'll want to be coming with us."

"This is blackmail. I have a home. People who count on me to—"

"Yeah, us. Three," he'd led her most of the way to the SUV. "I have no intention of letting you out of my sight anytime soon."

When all she did was squawk in protest, he figured it was his best opportunity. He leaned down and kissed her.

She didn't hit him.

Good sign.

She didn't even complain.

Better.

Then she kissed him back.

Oh yeah.

CHAPTER 9

Bude was a long, frustrating day, and Katie was ragged by the time the sun was going down.

Five cables from the US, one each from Canada and Africa, and one that stretched all of the way from India came ashore at Bude. They'd surveyed the landing points of the four at Widemouth Bay and the four more at Crooklets Beach as well as they could.

It had taken much of the afternoon, but they'd even managed to locate the new landing point for the 2Africa cable that Ricardo and Isobel had been so interested in.

Isobel had explained. "It's the world's newest major cable. It won't go live for a year or so, but it lands right here. This was our secondary mission. Once we understood the FLAG cables, we were to very carefully assess the risks to 2Africa. The question is, are we the only ones interested in it?"

Anton had peeked into all sorts of places they wouldn't have been able to get to otherwise...too bad he couldn't see underground.

She'd caught hints of Chas Thorstad, but nothing strong enough to trace.

Throughout the day, the team had kept asking her questions to which she had none of the answers.

Did her signals degrade with time, like Anton's ability to return to places?

Did repeated visits reinforce what she could sense?

How far away?

How certain?

What if—

She didn't have the answers to any of their questions, though she could almost feel the tracks of them circling around and around in the car. Each question almost a living thing, piling on top of all of the ones she had herself.

It just kept building and building until she felt as if she'd explode.

Michelle held out a water bottle, "Want one?"

It was one question too many and Katie felt as if her brain had just shredded.

"Bugger off! Okay? All of you, just bugger the bloody hell off."

Michelle sat frozen in shock, still holding out the water bottle.

The questions, piled on top of all of the marginal- to non-results, and the fact that she'd slept one hour of the last thirty-six—that with her head on Anton's shoulder as they'd raced north from Skewjack to Bude with the dawn (which was it's own weirdness)—had simply become too freaking much.

There was a stunned silence.

They'd been driving quietly from Crooklets Beach toward the Bude antenna farm where the cables were gathered together just like at Skewjack. In fact, Skewjack's big cables were probably routed up to here.

"Stop this bleeding car!"

Before it had fully stopped she was out the door and on the move. She didn't know or care where.

Away. It was all that mattered.

She could *feel* Anton close behind her.

Katie spun on him and he nearly ran her down.

"You especially. Just bugger off. And don't be following me with your weirdo creepy vision thing."

She saw the flash of pain slam into him. Saw him swallow it down like bitter medicine that just sat there and burned, but she couldn't find the words to take it back.

Instead she spun and plunged into a sheep field, not caring what she did or didn't step in. Sheep and lambs scattered before her like a bow wave, bleating in panic.

She testing her own reaction like probing a stinging tooth with the tip of her tongue.

She still didn't care.

The balance finally tipped between Katie's need to get away and her need to collapse, as she passed a long copse of trees. She ducked under the verge and dropped to the soil.

Southwest slope.

Bluebells.

Her eyes automatically tracked through the dim evening light, picking out the trail and the distinctive markings of a badger sett. Badgers dug long tunnels and the dirt had to go somewhere. Typically it created a defensive mound straight out of the tunnel. One of the proofs that it was a badger hole was their distinctive track —out of the hole, then a hard right or left turn to get clear. A more agile fox would come right over the top of the mound to look around.

There were also multiple holes, just three rather than the big clan by the airport that had ten easily visible tunnels, but more than a fox would typically create.

Sure enough, a black-and-white head peered at her from around the left side of a dirt mound.

"Just ignore me. Please," she begged it.

After some further consideration, it finally did and continued about its business.

"Sorry. That's not going to happen." Isobel had come straight up her path.

"Please just go away."

In answer, Isobel sat down in the dirt beside her. Apparently the badger was even less worried about Isobel than it had been about her own arrival.

"Was I so easy to find?"

"When you're radiating pain the way you are, it creates a beacon that I have a very hard time blocking out. But, like you, I have to get fairly close to feel those emotions. Once I do, then I can play Anton's warmer-cooler game and follow the emotion's intensity to its source."

"One more way of saying that you're not going to let me run away." Katie flopped back on the dirt and stared up at the leaves. The last of the daylight flickered through the canopy. The sun was low enough that the light never reached the ground, but it remained high enough to still dapple the beech leaves.

Isobel offered one of her beatific smiles that made her so hard to dismiss, but Katie was definitely in a dismissing mood. Before she could do so, Isobel spoke up.

"If you want to run away from us, I can't think of a reason to stop you. The hours are nuts. We used to wait months for an assignment to come up that needed our special skills. Now they seem to happen too often. The last movie, I barely learned the script before I shot it. That's not how I like to work."

Katie listened to the additional badgers starting to scrabble around the sett on the slope above them, but couldn't find the energy to look.

One, two, three…and four cubs.

Except even Tom Brown Jr. wasn't a good enough tracker to count a clan of badgers based solely on sound.

She tipped her head back into the dirt to look upside-down up the hill. On cue, three big heads and four small ones popped out of the different entrances and set about cleaning the area.

Katie flopped back to the ground.

"Bugger all," she murmured to herself.

"Indeed," Isobel agreed. "When there is a mission, the hours are awful and sometimes the dangers become very real, very fast. We don't have two Delta Force operators, a Night Stalker helicopter pilot, another Army pilot, and a paramedic just for the fun of it."

"Then why are you here, lady? Because I'm most

certainly running away from all that. I can hail a lorry to get me back home. Thanks so much for proving that all of my diligent training was utterly meaningless, by the way. Now would you very much mind buggering off?"

Isobel pulled up her knees and rested her chin on her crossed arms.

"I would think that we've proven that your skills are even more meaningful than you thought. Not only are you a highly skilled tracker for all of the reasons that have so impressed Ricardo and Hannah—which is not easy to do—but you've proven that you can reach beyond those skills. You've also shown immense adaptability today. But none of that is my point."

Katie blinked in surprise. "I think you just busted up your recruiting pitch."

"Do you know why I ended up in charge of Shadow Force: Psi?"

"Because you're a brilliant, beautiful, empath?"

"Close. Because I can feel people's feelings, I can help them find what's best for them, even when they don't know."

"Oh, so I should blindly to follow *you?* This isn't some lark; this is my life." Katie did her best to pay attention to the badgers and not to Isobel.

"Precisely. So when are you going to stop running away from it? When are you going to face the shitty package that your parents handed you, make your own choices, and move on?"

Katie jolted upright. "What do you know about my parents?"

Isobel stood and walked back out from under the trees.

Against her better judgement, Katie scrambled to follow.

Out from beneath the trees, the sunset was descending into St. George's Channel with a splash of reds and golds. A pair of green herons lazily glided across the sky, heading for their inland roost after a day of fishing. Even after they'd gone by, she could still feel them. They didn't so much impinge on her thoughts as they flew through her awareness if she focused on them. Rather, they were soft, no more significant than the sunlight.

She shook herself. "My parents?"

Isobel faced her. "I don't think you understand what we are. What you are. To the best of our knowledge, you are the seventh person that the entire US government knows about—anywhere—with a verifiable psi power. The secrecy of this unit is such that there are only four other people, all on a ranch in Montana, who know of our existence. They're our operational command. They take on missions and we accomplish them. We're still in the trial stage, but we're getting better. We've had to."

"But you're telling this to a total stranger."

Isobel smiled. "First, many people underestimate my gift. I may know more about what kind of a person you are than perhaps even you do. And that would be before I called you in, and our command gave you a clean bill of health—a very detailed clean bill of health. This is an exceedingly elite team and we're very careful. Mr. Brown sends his compliments, by the way, and no, he doesn't know why he received a call from our colonel. Of course, he isn't stupid either."

Tom, for all his quirks, was the closest thing she had to a real father. And he was *very* not stupid.

"He asked us to ask if you'd 'found your trail' yet."

Have ta find your own trail, lass. How many hundred times had he said that to her? Yet each summer, with nowhere else to go, she'd gone back to his tracker school, still no closer to finding an answer to his question.

The only reason she wasn't planning to return this year was because she couldn't afford the plane ticket without touching the allowance that her parents had been dumping into her bank account since the day she'd left for boarding school. It now constituted a small fortune, and she doubted they were even aware that it was still being augmented every month. Or that they cared one way or the other. It would be pocket change to them.

"And what trail do you see that haven't I found yet?" She tried to put heat into it, but it came out more like a child's whisper. She was fairly sure she didn't want to know.

"You know what makes a great movie?"

"A good script?"

Isobel chuckled. "That helps. It's the people. From the key grip to the stand-in to the star and director. I won't do a film unless it's with good people. That's one of the reasons my career has been so exceptional, because I can tell ahead of time if they're the kind of people I want to be working with."

Katie glanced back across the sheep's meadow to where the SUV was still parked along the side of the country lane. Some were standing around. But Anton, no longer identifiable in the descending evening light except by his size, sat atop one of the stone walls with his head bowed.

"But how do you *know?*"

Isobel rested a hand on Katie's arm. "Just one of the unexpected benefits of my gift. Emphasis on *gift.*" Then she walked up the path, leaving Katie to decide on her next action. If she'd missed the last coach to Mousehole, she had a couple friends in Bude. She could walk to her friends in under an hour and get her real life back.

Whereas in the other direction...

CHAPTER 10

Anton's hands ached from keeping them clenched as he sat on the stone wall, hunched with his elbows on his knees.

Even Michelle had come over and tried being nice to him.

"She didn't mean it, Anton. She's just hurt and scared."

When he'd bit back at her with, "Says the freak to the freak," all she did was hug him long and hard.

"Shit, Missy." He'd managed not to cry on her shoulder, but it had been too fucking close.

Now all he could do was sit and wait for Katie to walk away from him. The only woman for him was going to have to be another freak. But over the last forty-eight hours he'd finally learned what he wanted. It was someone a hell of a lot like Katie Whitfield, which experience had taught him was a very rare commodity.

He didn't give a goddamn if she chose to never sense another person, and demoted her gift to the category of a warped parlor trick.

But he couldn't turn his vision off. Not and be who he was.

He'd loved having that since he was a little boy. Being bad and sitting in the corner was no real punishment because he could just leave and go look at things elsewhere. He couldn't *do* things, like join in someone else's game, but he could sneak up on a toad or a deer until they were practically touching noses. Even cats didn't twig to him being there and so he'd figured he was truly invisible until he'd met Katie.

If he ever needed a better view while he was flying, he could just go sit on the top of the helo and look around. The swing of the main rotors didn't matter because he wasn't there to be hit.

Anton *liked* who he was and what he could do.

But why did it have to drive every single woman he ever liked right out the door?

Not that he was in love with Katie Whitfield. Because no matter what the storybooks said, it didn't happen that fast. Well, Jesse and Hannah had. But that had been under fire in the Honduran jungle. Ricardo and Michelle had a ton of history before they got together. And they almost didn't have a choice once they'd discovered how to link telepathically, yet it had still taken them most of a year.

Now there was just himself and Isobel. And she wasn't for him. He guessed that since he was such a damned mess, which she'd be able to sense, that he wasn't for her either.

For him there just had to be someone like—

A pair of battered sneakers came to a stop where he'd

been staring down at the grass until it was lost in the darkness.

He didn't even have to look ankle high to know it was her. Only Katie would stand right in front of him with her thoughts so clear that he could almost hear them like a Michelle-Ricardo telepath thing.

Almost.

But not quite.

He looked up at her face, as much as he could see of it in the descending darkness.

"Can you do me a favor, Anton?"

"If you're asking me to forget that I'm a freak—"

She shook her head.

"If you're asking me to forget you, that's not gonna be any more likely."

She shook her head again.

"If you're—"

"If you don't shut up, I'll never get the nerve to say what I'm trying to say."

Anton almost laughed. "Okay, right. Shutting up. Not good at that when I'm nervous."

She touched his arm briefly, but drew it back before he could think whether or not he was supposed to take her hand.

He resisted the urge to shift over to his vision—it was much better than normal sight at night—but checking out her expression, when she couldn't see him back, didn't seem very fair.

"I'm really new to this." He could hear her take a deep breath. "I don't have any idea what I'm doing."

Because he couldn't think of what to say, he prompted her with a grunt when she paused.

"Just know…that…I'm looking for my path. I have no idea what it looks like or where it leads, but the fact that there might actually be one for me is more than I ever knew before."

"Katie, do you want to walk the, uh, start of that path with…" he couldn't quite say "me" so he asked, "…us?"

He could just make out her nod.

Anton wanted to get up and dance. He wanted to wrap his arms around her and just hold on. Instead, he spoke as softly as the night.

"I'd like that, Katie. I'd like that a lot."

When she nodded again, he rose slowly and side by side they headed over to the SUV.

A trail begins, Katie reminded herself. *It progresses. The important task isn't to interpret the trail's intent. The important task is to follow it in the moment and see where it leads.* It was the closest thing she had to a mantra.

But in all of her years of training and working as a guide, she hadn't expected it to lead to a highly secure government site.

Once she and Anton climbed back into the SUV, they'd finished the short drive to the Bude antenna site.

Compared to the Skewjack building, GCHQ Bude was *intensely* secure. It was one of the signal-gathering stations of the Government Communications Headquarters—the equivalent of America's NSA.

Ever since the First World War they'd been the codebreaking arm of the United Kingdom. They'd run Bletchley Park where Germany's Enigma Code had been broken, significantly changing the course of World War II for the better.

And in 2013, Edward Snowden had revealed that they were listening to all of the trans-Atlantic cable traffic right here—though she still didn't know why everyone had acted so surprised.

The UK's center for processing the signals from undersea cables lay just five klicks north of Bude itself, maybe seven by the winding country lane that passed the gate. Perched a hundred meters back from the coastal cliffs, GCHQ's installation covered a half-kilometer square. Twenty-one giant radio dish antennas were pointed toward different portions of the sky. Were they listening to Russian satellite transmissions or sending coded messages to the Americans because they knew better than to trust the undersea cables?

There was little evidence of the cables reaching here. Except for the patched slice in the one-lane country road. For kilometer after kilometer, the half-meter wide patch stretched along the road. It was broken only occasionally by securely locked, square manhole covers. Some bore the markings of some phone company or Internet provider. But some had acronyms she didn't recognize. It made her wonder what else she'd driven across over the years without realizing.

She'd never really had reason to think about the undersea cables beyond the occasional naming contest in a Cornish pub. It was a whole layer of her world that she'd never thought to track before.

The road ran close beside the eastern double fence, four meters high with razor wire along the top and a ten-meter-wide no-man's-land between them.

"I don't think you'll be slipping in there," she teased Hannah. Hannah spoke the least of the team's women. Michelle was overwhelming, and Anton was right, Isobel was a little scary. Hannah's silence actually made her the easiest for Katie to be comfortable around.

Ricardo, in the back with Michelle and Isobel, must have overheard her. He grunted noncommittally, as if maybe it was possible for a Delta Force operator to penetrate even the antenna farm's security.

Hannah drove a few long moments more, then cricked her neck before answering. "It would depend a lot on whether there are cut-sensors in the fence, or if it's just a mesh. I'd bet on the former, though probably just for the inner line. It takes a lot of effort to bypass. Also, knowing the types of ground sensors buried in the no man's land, mapping the camera sweeps and patrol timings… That sort of thing."

That sort of thing.

Katie decided she'd be better off tracking various wildlife and lost dogs (her other major source of minor income). This was the first time in a long time she'd agreed to track anything human.

She'd joined Tom on a few lost-kid hunts. Once they'd found the kid lost in the woods. A second kid's trail had ended in a set of car tracks that had disappeared untraceably onto a highway. The final one had ended with a daughter-mother murder-suicide. She'd been the tracker on point for that search, making her the first to see them. She'd sworn to never track people again.

Yet here she was. Sodding Chas Thorstad!

Anton's leg had brushed against hers as they came near the station. It was their first contact since she'd raged at him. It was a nice peace offering. She appreciated its thoughtfulness and left her knee brushing against his.

They were well past the station when she felt it. Not like an electric shock, but rather like she'd been walking on solid ground one instant and was suddenly knee deep in a peat bog without warning.

She pulled back instinctively. Getting mired in a peat bog could be a deadly mistake.

But they were past it and the feeling was gone.

"Chas. We just crossed his path. Turn around. Back up. Something."

Hannah did as she was told.

But it wasn't there.

"It was so strong just a moment ago."

Anton reached out a hand, found her thigh in the dark inside the car, which was surprisingly forward.

But she felt…something.

Then he tugged lightly sideways bringing their knees back together.

Her initial reaction had pulled her knee away from Anton's—and the feeling had instantly disappeared.

Now, Katie brushed her knee back against his and the feeling returned.

And there it was again.

When she tried to see his face by the dashboard lights

and the spillover from the antenna farm's security lights, he appeared to be studying the back of Jesse's passenger-seat headrest.

"Talk to me, Katie." She'd think later how she felt about those being his first words to her since the stone wall.

"Where are you?"

"The southeast corner of the security fence. There's a coastal walking path that runs close along this side of the fence."

"He was there." Anton's vision must have "gotten out" earlier and started walking the fence line.

"I'm gonna take me a stroll along the path. Let me know if he fades away," Anton spoke softly. "You can keep driving, Hannah. Won't bother me none."

Hannah drove until all except the largest ten-meter antenna dishes were out of sight behind them before finding a narrow pullout along the lane.

"Are you sure it's him?" Isobel asked from the back seat.

"He feels like…a slime mold. Why didn't I notice that before?" Then she answered her own question. "Because I didn't think the feeling was associated with anything outside my own head. I was— Right there, Anton! It just got weaker, so back up a step." He must have because the feeling was back again.

"That's the end of his path."

"Okay, I'm going to walk in a circle. Let me know if he pops back up."

Katie sat there in the seat beside Anton, her knee brushing his, and wished she didn't feel.

Wait!

When *had* Anton placed his knee against hers? No contact since she'd run off into the fields and found the second badger sett.

Then just as they came up to the antenna farm, he'd put his knee up against hers—to go on one of his vision-walk things.

"You bloody bastard!" Katie tried to just say it only to Anton but the stopped car was too quiet.

Hannah and Jesse twisted around to look at her and she could feel the other three behind, studying her intently.

"What?" "Why?" "Who?"

Unsure who to answer, she targeted Anton, shoving against his arm as if she could push him away inside the confines of the car.

"You're just using me!"

"What? No. I wasn't."

"Up your blooming arse!"

"Katie! What are you talking about?"

Just then she felt Chas-the-bog again, rather than Anton-the-arsehole. "There. You just crossed his path again." She couldn't believe she was still helping him.

But when she tried to yank her knee away, his hand still held her in position. He wasn't restraining her; it was just that his strength was so massive even a casual touch pinned her leg in place.

"An*ton!*"

"Wait! Just wait! I don't know what's going on."

She yanked her knee free of his clasp and the Chas feeling disappeared again.

Anton blinked hard and turned to actually look at her.

"You were just using me, arsehole!" She felt it was necessary to repeat herself now that all of him was here.

The others in the car were dead silent. If Isobel tried to mediate, Katie might just turn around and smack her at this moment—international film star or not.

"No, I wasn't. Well yes. But… What are you talking about?"

"I'm talking about this," she batted her knee against his and then pulled away.

No blink feeling of Chas-the-bog when their knees touched, but then Anton was no longer out there; he was here.

"I thought you—" Katie thought about all of the others listening in and decided that she didn't give a good goddamn. "—were showing that you liked me. Leaning your knee against mine."

"Sounds cozy to me," Jesse made it a mollifying statement.

"Shut up, cowboy!" Katie snapped at him.

"But I *do* like you," Anton protested.

"Yet still you were using me to find Chas!" She scrabbled for the door handle in the dark, when his hand landed heavily on her shoulder pinning her butt to the seat.

"Katie," he leaned over until their noses were close enough together that she'd have bit his if she was a different woman. "I like you a great deal. I brushed my knee against yours because I like you. I did it before I went lookabout because I like feeling you beside me when I can't see you."

Katie took a deep breath, which didn't help much. "You swear that it wasn't on the off chance that I'd feel Chas through you?"

"Can't say that I thought about it until you called out that you felt him. I was just going out to see what I could see."

Michelle leaned forward and whispered by Katie's ear, "As much as I hate to say anything in support of my semi-demi-dram-brother, Anton is a real be-here-now kind of guy. Doesn't think ahead a whole lot. If he had more than half a brain... Well, he doesn't, so you'll never have to worry much about ulterior motives with him."

Katie wanted to ask Isobel to use her empathic ability to verify what Anton was saying. Her own attempts at relationships never lasted long, so trusting her own judgement was hard. She'd long ago decided that she was simply better off alone.

"Really, Anton?"

For a moment, she thought she saw his smile flash in the darkness, then he leaned in and kissed her.

It wasn't like the first time in the dark at Skewjack Farm—all heat and fun. Now it was soft and filled with questions.

Questions she didn't have any answers to, but she certainly enjoyed the kiss.

CHAPTER 11

Anton lay awake in his bed at the Ship Inn.

He'd had no sleep in two nights, and now it was noon in Mousehole. Which was seven a.m. in San Antonio, by which time he'd be finishing his morning workout and scouting around for breakfast. His body definitely didn't know which way was up.

And his thoughts wouldn't shut up.

It wasn't the kind of problem he normally had. As a kid, Michelle would lose a night's sleep, or several nights' worth when she was worrying at something. He'd always felt that it was his brotherly duty to rub in the fact that it never happened to him.

But now, when exhaustion should have dragged him under long ago, his thoughts were swirling.

He'd tried pretending it was analyzing the mission.

It had shifted like slippery ice. One moment their assignment was about testing the various cables' security in the UK. And the next it was about just who Chas Thorstad might be and what in tarnation he was up to.

Colonel Gibson had probably started them out on the wrong beach intentionally, just to see how long it would take the average person to unravel what was going on. But they weren't the average team, especially not since he'd spotted Katie watching the badgers. Without that, they might not have picked up on Chas as a target.

Chance?

Yet chance had played strongly in Shadow Force: Psi's favor more than seemed likely. He was sure that Isobel would have some deep thoughts on that, but he had no idea what they could be.

Chance or whatever weird force that was acting in their favor had also brought Katie into their circle. He had no more complaints about that than a hound dog at a hamburger joint.

He sighed.

No *real* question about what was keeping him awake.

Chas Thorstad could have a ship's mast up his butt for all Anton cared.

Katie Whitfield. Damn but that woman had the sweetest kiss. He'd wanted to invite her back to his room when they returned to Mousehole. Or maybe he should have offered to escort her to hers to…make sure she got back safely? Like Mousehole was such a dangerous place. The main hazard he saw was a chance of collapsing into a state of semi-bucolic bliss and never moving again.

But if he had, maybe she would have invited him in.

Or was it too soon?

Or—

"Shit but you're a mess, Anton Bowman." No one argued with his assessment.

Sleep.

If he could just stop thinking and sleep, then he'd—

A fist thumped on his door. He'd recognize Michelle's graceless knock anywhere. She didn't just breeze into his room.

"Yo." He was too tired to do more, but it was enough.

She swung the door just partway open, then peeked in carefully. "You're alone."

"Don't sound so damned surprised."

"Why didn't you just jump her?" Michelle came the rest of the way in and sat at the foot of his bed.

"Because I'm a decent, thoughtful kind of guy."

"Since when?"

"Since…" Well, he tried to be decent and thoughtful, though he'd never found it difficult to entice a woman into his bed. Since he'd never found a reason to complain about it, he took happy advantage of it. Typically. "Since this time?"

Michelle made a thoughtful humming tone deep in her throat, but didn't elaborate.

"Why aren't you sleeping, or screwing Ricardo?"

"Did the latter," she bragged, "then was doing the former when Ricardo rousted me."

"So he's insatiable. Congratulations."

"He is," she rubbed it in, "and so am I, so that works. But he woke me telepathically. He, Hannah, and Katie were patrolling the town. They found where Chas Thorstad was staying."

That had Anton sitting up. The room only spun a little from lack of sleep. "So bust his ass and find out what he's up to."

"Where he *was* staying. He's bolted."

"Aw shit." Anton flopped back onto the bed.

"But the landlady overheard where he was going. Wouldn't talk to us, of course, but she and Katie go way back."

Anton waited, knowing Michelle wouldn't be able to resist telling him.

"Time to go back to the motherland, semi-demi-dram-bro."

"San Antonio? Damn but that's great news." For that, he'd get up and pack right now—awful plane ride be damned.

"Dakar, Senegal."

He had to think to even remember where the hell that was.

"Westernmost tip of the bulge into the Atlantic," Michelle said it like he was an idiot.

"West Africa, I knew that." At least he was pretty sure he had at some point. "That's not the motherland. Pa's people were from..." He couldn't remember. He remembered that they'd arrived a century before American Independence.

"Goree," Michelle provided.

"Right. That's what Grandma Bowman traced us back to."

"Traced *you,* Anton. Remember we're not related. Goree Island was the slave trading post in Dakar, Senegal."

"Oh," he shrugged. He'd never been particularly hyped on family history. He was far more bothered by Michelle declaring they weren't related. He wanted to ask her about Katie, but now she'd made it feel all weird. "When are we out of here?"

She looked at her watch. "Let's see. Ricardo woke me up about an hour ago. Hannah got us a flight out of Land's End Airport about ten minutes after that. So you'd better pack fast, you've got about five minutes, then we leave without you."

"Goddamn it, Missy. You've known for an hour and you give me five minutes notice?" He shoved up out of bed and hurried to the dresser to pack.

He was half done when reality slammed in.

They were leaving.

And Michelle hadn't even left him time to track down Katie and say goodbye.

He spun to face the door, but his stepsister was already gone.

God damn it! He wished they really *weren't* related.

"Do you have a yellow fever vaccination?"

"Um, yes." Katie didn't know why Hannah was asking. She'd barely gotten back to her room after they'd figured out where Chas had gone before Hannah had knocked on her door.

As soon as they'd found out Chas had left town she knew it was over. Shadow Force: Psi would be moving on, and she'd be getting her life back. She was far too exhausted to decide if it was a good thing or a bad one.

"How light do you travel?"

"Pretty light," she pointed at her field pack.

Travel? Her whole *life* fit in there. With room to spare. Was that traveling light or living like the nomad she'd become? She felt as if she left even less impression on the Earth than when she was wearing her moccasins.

Tracking wasn't a high-equipment career: a GPS device backed up by a good compass just in case, batteries, water bottles, and sunscreen. Her one luxury was her night-vision monocular, but she didn't need more than small, lightweight binoculars. A couple changes of clothes and some foul-weather gear.

All she had to show for a life.

No villa in Nice. No apartment in New York. No multi-floor condo right in London's core. None of the trappings her parents considered so essential to maintain their status—the only thing they really cared about.

"Do you have a current passport?"

Katie nodded, still not awake enough to figure out what was going on.

"Isobel wants to know how you feel about traveling with us for a bit?"

"To..." she recalled what Dora had said about overhearing Chas's destination. Classic Dora, her best friend jumped straight to the wrong conclusion. She was the one who had sent Chas to her when he'd asked about a guide. Now she "sensed" that Katie had finally discovered her soulmate in Chas Thorstad and the universe wanted her to chase after him. Which, she realized, was exactly what Hannah was asking her to do. At least the chasing-after part.

To Dakar?

With Shadow Force: Psi?

Was that a journey she wanted to risk? Hope had never been more than a dangerous companion. Some overly needy sliver of her soul thought about what it would be like spending time with these people. Hanging with three of the most amazing women she'd ever met.

Even now, Hannah's patience as Katie tried to process the options revealed a deep kindness.

And then there was Anton.

It was pretty obvious what direction their relationship was headed if they spent more time together. She'd thought seriously about following him to Ship Inn before Hannah had pulled her aside and started asking about where Chas was staying.

Was that something she wanted?

There was no point in thinking about it lasting. But did she want it to even start?

A trail begins, Katie remembered. *It progresses. The important task isn't to interpret the trail's intent. The important task is to follow it in the moment and see where it leads.*

She pushed to her feet. "How long do I have?"

"Enough time, just be quick," then Hannah was gone.

CHAPTER 12

Anton was the first to reach their car parked out on the Mousehole breakwater—no parking along the narrow streets near Ship Inn.

Fifteen minutes later, he was still sitting on the seawall when Jesse showed up.

"If you're thinking getting here so fast earns you a seat up front beside my wife, you got some rethinking to do there, pard."

"Just trying to show you up, you lazy cowboy. Don't you ever move above a mosey?" That's when Anton figured out that Michelle had been messing with him, giving him plenty of warning but telling him he didn't have any time.

Time that he could have used saying goodbye to—

He spotted Michelle's jaunty stride coming around the turn of the breakwater.

Anton pushed to his feet and strode up to her until he blocked her way toe-to-toe.

"Hey, you're early," she grinned at him, enjoying her joke.

"You fucking bitch!"

She blinked in surprise and stumbled backward.

He stepped right up to her again. "You couldn't just tell me I had plenty of time, could you? So damned pleased with your goddamn games that I lost the chance to go find Katie and at least say goodbye."

Michelle's face shifted to horror. It took all of his restraint to not grab her by the throat and toss her off the seawall.

"Didn't think of that, did you?"

"Oh God, Anton. I'm so sorry. I didn't. I swear I never would—"

"Done, Michelle. I'm just so goddamn done with you."

She opened her mouth in shock, but the only sound to come out was a small squeak of distress.

He turned away, past where Jesse waited by the car. Anton leaned on the seawall and stared out to sea. He couldn't bear to turn and face Mousehole.

Katie was there…somewhere. Behind him. In the town he'd never had a chance to explore.

No way in hell would she forgive him for simply disappearing.

Maybe if he'd thought to write her a note, the Ship Inn's bartender could have delivered it for him. Not that he'd ever been all that magical with the written word, but goddamn it, he would have tried.

He didn't even have her number. No way to find her.

She'd sleep off the last thirty-six hours, wake up to find him gone, and write him off forever. She'd know for a fact that he'd totally used her to find Chas' path out by the Bude antenna farm, no matter how much that wasn't true. Katie Whitfield would *hate* him and he'd never find a way to explain otherwise.

He heard the others arrive, but no one bothered him. Which was a good thing because it saved him from drowning any of his friends in the harbor.

Anton didn't even know how he'd get in the same car with Michelle. Christ, he wouldn't even be able to go home for Ma's holiday dinners. Those were the highlight of his entire *year.* But if Michelle was there, no way could he even go home.

And she and Ricardo were a third of Shadow Force: Psi. Was he going to lose Shadow Force too? He'd left the US Army to be a part of this team. Would they take him back? God he hoped so.

"Anton," Ricardo called out.

Oh right. And he'd be losing his best friend too while he was at it.

"Here's the last of us. Let's saddle up."

Maybe he should jump ship right here and now.

No question about it really.

He told himself to be civil, but he wouldn't be taking any bets.

Anton turned from the sea to say goodbye. To change his life, again.

"Sorry if I took too long," Katie said as she walked around the hood of the car. A true outdoorsman's pack sat lightly on her back. She wore her boots, shorts, a denim blouse, and her glorious hair spilling loose over her shoulders like dark sunlight.

He'd never seen a more amazing sight.

Anton didn't have any words.

When she stopped and dropped her pack, he simply stepped forward and wrapped her in his arms. Resting his cheek on her hair, he breathed her in, and held on for all he was worth.

Any questions Katie had about whether or not traveling with the team was a good choice were washed away in Anton's embrace.

He didn't just hold her, he wrapped her in his big arms and crushed her against his chest. More intimate than either of their kisses, he didn't ease up, but kept holding her until she was having trouble breathing.

"Um, hi. Do you always greet new team members this way?"

"Just you," he whispered into her hair.

"You do know that we saw each other just two hours ago. Not that I'm complaining."

"Seems longer."

"You can let go of me now."

He gave her a final squeeze that really did knock away the last of her air, then eased her back just enough to look down at her.

She could see a dozen questions in his eyes. "You going to ask another moccasin question?"

He just shook his head. "You're coming with us?"

"Isobel seemed to think it was a good idea."

That earned her another one of his gloriously crushing

hugs.

"I guess you do, too."

She could feel his nod, then he finally let her go.

As she stepped away from him, Katie saw Michelle sidle up to him carefully. Not since her initial fumble at their first meeting had she seen Michelle be anything other than utterly confident. Katie had never once felt that confident for two minutes in a row.

But right now, Michelle looked as scared as a rabbit as she stood in front of Anton's looming height.

As Katie bent down to retrieve her pack from where she'd dropped it on the granite pier, she was just barely close enough to hear Michelle's words.

"You know I'd never hurt you on purpose, Anton."

"Yeah, I guess I know that. Doesn't make it hurt any less, Missy. It was a damned shitty thing to do."

They both stood there awkwardly. If anyone else noticed what was going on, they were kind enough to not be watching.

Katie didn't know if it was her place or even what was going on, but at Michelle's obvious distress she couldn't help herself. She got Anton's attention and mouthed clearly, "Hug her."

When Anton finally did, Michelle lay her face on his shoulder and started to cry.

Katie looked away to give them their privacy.

She'd just finished stowing her pack when Isobel spoke softly beside her.

"You done good, Katie Whitfield. Knew you would."

Katie didn't know anything of the kind, but she also knew she'd never received higher praise.

CHAPTER 13

Anton didn't outright die on the flight to Dakar, but after six hours in economy—the only seats available on such short notice—he sort of wished he had. Not as badly as the hour-long hop from Cornwall to London in the tiny commuter plane, but very, very close.

The only highlight was that Katie had sat next to him. But instead of getting to know her better, she'd put her head on his shoulder and passed out for the entire flight.

While he'd been totally charmed, and enjoyed being able to rest his cheek on her hair—until he got a crick in his neck to go with the ache in his back and the throbbing in his knees—he was also ticked that everyone else seemed able to sleep on the flight.

Almost everyone. He got some satisfaction from seeing Jesse also suffer. His six-three didn't fit in economy all that much better than Anton's six-five. They exchanged a few grimaces across the aisle about the women sleeping so peacefully against their shoulders, but mostly they both stared straight ahead and focused on pain management.

The Senegalese airport was very neat and modern. It had only three jetways, which were apparently reserved for Air France flights or something. Their British Airways flight was parked well out on the tarmac and they were bused into the terminal.

For perhaps the first time in his life, Anton didn't feel completely out of place. At six-five, he was far from the tallest black men on the bus. Most were long, lean, and the average skin was even darker than his own, but mostly it was a relief to not always be looking down on a sea of heads. Even many of the women topped six feet.

The men were almost universally in black slacks, well-polished black shoes, with a button-down white shirt.

The women were a cloud of wild and wonderful prints. Just watching them, he could understand why so many people in the States went for "ethnic" even if they were no more recently African than he was. Blues, golds, reds, greens...they all flourished in such massive and cheery prints that it was impossible not to smile. He also didn't mind that Senegalese fashion apparently dictated that they wear their clothing very tight, revealing splendid shapes and curves.

"Bet you'd look good in some of those getups," he whispered down to Katie.

"As if. Do they even make clothes for short people here?" Her head was below the heights of most people's shoulders, so he kissed the top of it.

One of the men, making a far more discreet show of

flexing his sore legs than Anton was, offered him a smile and said something in a quick language.

"I thought they spoke French here," Michelle said close by his elbow. Her gangly five-ten didn't stand out here at all.

"Doesn't help. I don't speak French." Michelle had tried to teach him when they were kids, but it just seemed to bounce off his ears without ever reaching his memory.

"I am sorry," the man apologized in French-accented English. "Your face. I assumed you spoke Wolof."

"Wolof?" Maybe this *was* where his family had been enslaved from if a local identified him as that familiar looking.

"Senegal is a land of many voices. Mouths?" the man continued.

"Tongues."

"Tongues, yes. Thank you. Wolof is the common tongues. Many, especially here in the city, speak French. It is our language of business. Many, many, we now learn English like me."

"You're doing really well," Michelle thought to say. She might be sharp-tongued, especially to him, but she was a decent person. Which was always a bit of surprise when she did something to remind him of that.

"I am learning." The man smiled an acknowledgement. Neither self-deprecating nor boasting, it was a simple statement.

Then he, Michelle, and Katie began chattering away in French, and he looked greatly relieved. In fact, he looked very much as if he'd like to take Katie home despite Anton standing right here. Michelle had a ring on her finger but Katie didn't have that kind of defense yet.

Yet?

Someone should smack him with a two-by-four—hard.

At the terminal, they were soon through security and had their luggage.

However, the short transit from the airport to the rental car lot disabused him of any idea that this was somehow normal. In the Army, he'd done his tours in Iraq and Afghanistan, but he wasn't ready for the abrupt change that happened outside these airport doors.

In Southwest Asia, he'd flown into shitty secure airfields and deployed into the sprawl of shitty secure American base housing. He flew Black Hawks with far more holes than they were designed with. But he'd never before landed at a developing world civilian airport.

The newness of the airport lasted across the width of a frontage driveway, a twenty-car-deep parking lot, and a perimeter road. A meter beyond the far shoulder lay arid desert. The sun was so bright that it hurt through his sunglasses. It was only an hour past dawn and the heat was almost as blinding—he was sweating standing still. The air smelled of nothing but dust.

And they were instantly surrounded by guys on the hustle.

"Carry your bag?"

"Need a taxi?"

"From America? I'm Number One guide. Show you special places."

"I have special car, take you to city. Anywhere you go."

He pulled Katie close as their two Delta operators slipped quietly to the fore. With Hannah and Ricardo clearing the path, they were soon in their Ford Expedition SUV. It was weird to have exactly the same car in another country. Almost the same, the steering wheel had shifted from right to left and Hannah and Jesse had switched sides, but everything else was the same.

In minutes they were racing along the broad multi-lane highway to the west.

"Hey, this isn't so bad."

"Tomas," Katie raised her hand, palm down until her knuckles hit the roof, "the tall guy on the transport, said that the heat, dust, and humidity are early this year. They usually don't start for another month. Luckily, today is a mild day."

"This is mild? I'm screwed." Anton sighed. Born in North Carolina and now living in Texas, he should thrive on the heat. He didn't. He actually liked the few times he'd been in cooler places.

"You're screwed then," Katie agreed amiably.

Anton rolled his eyes at her and she offered one those trickling laughs. "Looked like that guy Tomas was hitting on you."

Michelle chimed in from the back seat, "Two marriage offers between the plane and the terminal and another one to live to together in sin. You're going to have to put a ring on her finger just to protect her in this place."

Anton could feel the blood drain from face.

Katie did her best to keep a straight face.

"Oh God. I did it again," Michelle groaned from the back seat.

Anton was studying the back of Jesse's head with great intensity.

It was just too much, and Katie lost it.

Everything that had been building up inside her: the uncertainty of how she was going to survive the year, her annexation by this team, whatever was going on between her and Anton that was somehow perfectly captured in Anton's half-panicked and deeply unsettled expression…

All of it just exploded forth.

The laughter started big and it just grew. She wrapped both hands around Anton's big biceps, leaned her forehead against his shoulder, and still couldn't find a way to get it under control.

There were other, uncertain laughs here and there drawn out by hers, but her own never slowed, like it was a spooked deer.

When it collapsed into breathless pain around her ribs and a dose of hiccups, Anton reached around to thump her on the back—which was ridiculously funny all over again.

She was about half-recovered when Anton rumbled out a deep, "What was that about?" Now he'd shifted to half-consoling and deeply confused. Hard to blame him.

Katie almost lost it again, but the last of the hiccups and the lack of air saved her. "I—"

Nope. Not enough air. She tried again.

"I just…pictured the last forty-eight hours of my life. Then thought about the next forty-eight."

He looked at her quizzically, but Hannah got the joke and offered a short snap of laughter as she slalomed through a cluster of battered orange and yellow taxis.

"Yeah, really? Right?" Katie asked her.

"Yeah, really," Hannah answered without any hint of laughter.

And that sobered Katie up hard.

No one else seemed to get the joke, so she tried to explain it.

"Two nights ago, I was taking a wildlife photographer to look at badgers. Since then, I've aided and abetted you all breaking into Skewjack. Using psi powers, *psi,* mind you, we're now tracking someone that you conjecture could be an international terrorist, to Senegal—on a completely different continent! So two nights from now am I going to be married and in love ever-after with an American ex-soldier most of a foot taller than I am? It's just a little much."

The men all laughed appreciatively, even Michelle.

Hannah's shrug said that wasn't a bad description of exactly what had happened to her. In a careful glance toward the back seat, Katie saw that Isobel wasn't laughing either. Almost as if she would be surprised if that *weren't* the case.

The important task isn't to interpret the trail's intent. The important task is to follow it in the moment and see where it leads.

Katie decided that she was definitely in over her head.

CHAPTER 14

Dakar had to be the craziest place Anton had ever been.

Unable to think about the idea of being married to a woman like Katie, because *c'mon,* stuff like that didn't happen to guys like him, he needed a distraction.

He concentrated instead on what was happening outside the window.

The highway raced across the landscape.

Now through desert dotted with crazy fat, white trees.

"Baobabs, like in *The Little Prince,*" Michelle said dreamily.

Katie echoed with a happy sigh.

Great! Now his girlfriend, if that's what Katie had become without him quite noticing, was bonding with his pain-in-the-ass stepsister. He wasn't sure if he was ready for the two of them to get along.

That soon gave way to a city…with no people. Three- and four-story concrete-block apartment buildings. A mall. A couple of hotels. A massive sports stadium.

Kilometer after kilometer of shops. A whole damned city that existed only along the highway with no people. Just one to two blocks behind all the new concrete was the land of red desert and baobab trees among the thorny acacia bushes.

There was the occasional bicycle, and twice a family walking along, but mostly it was a great void of ghost-city. And all of it, from the desert to the newest building, was covered in a patina of red dust. It was like a massive alien abduction had removed all the people and the dust was reclaiming the world.

After fifteen or twenty kilometers of this, it…snapped.

One moment he was watching the emptiness of an unoccupied city of colossal scale. The next they were in the hovel sprawl that he'd come to expect around the edges of urban centers, even American ones. In the space of a few minutes they plunged from ghost-city, through hovel-land, into central Dakar. If paint jobs, almost entirely in soft pastels, indicated that a building was finished, it seemed as if a third of the city was new construction. The gray of raw concrete-block rose at every turn.

And the city teemed with life despite the early hour. While they waited to clear the congestion at a roundabout, someone came up to his window and tried to sell him a new cellphone cover. She had a hundred or more dangling from strings in all sorts of designs and sizes. At the same time, Jesse was being offered a shining pair of Nikes, except the swoosh had been sewn on upside down.

Some of the sellers were independent. Others

appeared to be outward extensions of the tiny shops that lined either side of the road.

Through the window, he bought some surprisingly good coffees. A hundred meters on, he purchased crunchy French-style baguettes spread with Nutella for probably too many CFA notes, but he was okay with that as he just assumed he'd be paying the Westerner's price.

"Where do we even start?" Katie asked as if he'd have a clue.

"You're the hot, sexy tracker. You tell us."

Katie looked at him strangely.

"What?" Anton mumbled around a mouthful of baguette.

"I'll buy the hot because this is at least a thousand degrees hotter than Cornwall. But..." She could feel it prickling her skin it was so intense.

"Damn, Katie. Any man doesn't think you're sexy is an idiot."

That would be every man in her past. She looked down at herself. Boots, rugged shorts, and a denim work shirt that had seen too many seasons. Who was he trying to kid?

"Seriously, woman." Anton reinforced his judgement strongly enough that she almost believed that *he* believed what he was saying. But she knew better than to...

Path to nowhere. She did her best to chop off that line of thought.

A trail begins.

Where did this trail begin?

It started at sea.

Then—

"Cables come ashore. Let's follow the shoreline."

"Jesse," Hannah called out to her husband.

"On it," he had a tablet computer in his lap and was soon looking at a map.

No one questioned or doubted. Even when she was being the sole guide of a group, she'd always be questioned about whether or not she knew where she was going or how could she be sure this was the right way. Leading trainings for Tom's school, people would doubt that the "lass with charming British accent", as Tom always insisted on calling her, had a clue. It was a surprise to have the members of Shadow Force not even hesitate.

Jesse described the map for everyone else, "Dakar is like a big triangular peninsula. This highway is the primary connection to the city from the rest of the country. Take the next exit, then head left until you run into the ocean."

"Oh God," Anton groaned. "I'm going to be so lost. There's water in every direction again."

His wink and smile belied his tone, and actually made Katie feel even better. He reminded her of their brief time together in Cornwall. The fun moments in among the bewildering changes. His easy humor had been a constant thread throughout.

He'd also brought an incredible adventure her way. She'd only ever been to Europe and the US. Now she was on a brand-new continent. While she'd have preferred a nice cup of tea, she'd grown accustomed to Tom's penchant for bitter coffee as well. The Senegalese coffee was much lighter and it perfectly cut the heavy chocolate of the Nutella baguette.

As Hannah took them off the highway and jounced onto a rough, narrow street, she let the motion bounce her knee against Anton's once more. Despite the heat, she liked the feeling of connection. Not some weird psychic whatever, just the feeling of her knee brushing against his.

He looked at her questioningly.

A man who learned? That was a miracle in itself. "Just let me know when you go lookabout, okay?"

He nodded carefully.

Despite the heat, she kept the window down and breathed in the city. It was probably an ill-advised choice. The sky was thick with humidity and hazy with dust. It quickly formed a gritty layer on their skin as it stuck to the sunscreen that everyone had slathered on before leaving the airport.

The dust would be good for tracking across a very short period of time, but it would then quickly mask the very trail sign that it had captured. Tom had talked about how such things cut both ways.

Dakar had a thousand smells. A woman and a small boy were squatting by a small propane tank with a burner built into the top. From the large wok on the burner, she could smell the roasting peanuts. When the boy spotted her, he scrambled over and offered her several plastic bags of peanuts the size of a banger sausage. She pointed at three.

"Cinq mille," he informed her stoutly.

"Une mille," she held up one finger. A thousand CFA

was a little over one British pound. She didn't know what a fair price was, but she knew his first offer would be far too high.

He held up three fingers, she offered two. He took it and skipped back to his mother, who waved happily. Apparently she'd just been taken by the young entrepreneur, but didn't care.

She handed the peanuts around and went back to watching the city. The car jounced along the rough street only a little faster than a walk. Some sections of the road were paved, but small dunes of red sand, thick with plastic garbage and small chunks of concrete made for a rough ride.

A mango seller flourished mangos on a stout stick. She also had a big knife for peeling the fruit. The thick sweetness filled the air…until they rolled past a cow who raised its tail to deliver a massive flop of oozing brown that almost came in her window as Hannah squeezed the car past.

The people were impossibly clean and beautiful amidst all of the dust and debris. A laughing group of teenage schoolgirls sauntered by in their blue-skirt and white-blouse uniforms, well aware that they were the most beautiful females ever to walk on two legs.

Little children were everywhere and didn't seem to be attached to any one adult.

"Are they safe?"

It was Hannah who answered. "The society is very community-centric. A child doesn't just have parents, it has a hundred aunties watching out for it wherever it goes. If a child gets in trouble or needs a reprimand, someone will always be there. I did a three-week, cross-cultural training mission here early in my career."

Knowing the children were safe didn't make their carefree explorations any less surprising.

The traffic was thick and jostling. There were scooters and motorcycles weaving through the traffic. A three-wheeled bicycle with a large wooden delivery box on the back rolled effortlessly through the confusion. It stopped at a tiny store no bigger than her room back in Mousehole. She could only laugh when he lifted an armful of baguettes out of the box like so much kindling, and carried it into the store. A baker's delivery van.

She wasn't paying any mind as the big port, busy with a dozens of ships slipped by.

"Goree Island." Hannah pointed at an island beyond the harbor's mouth.

Michelle leaned forward and rested a hand on Anton's shoulder. "Pa said that's where your ancestors…" she cleared her throat. "Where your side of the family came through. Most likely from somewhere inland, but that's the last place they'd have touched the continent. It was the biggest slave trading spot in all of Africa."

"Huh. Okay, that's officially weird."

Katie looked out at the island and felt herself cringe inside. Her family wasn't *nouveau riche*. They were old English money, cotton merchant money that had driven the wool merchants almost to extinction. Cotton money meant their ships had traveled a triangle from England to Africa to pick up slaves, delivered them to America, then carried cotton bales back to England to feed the big British mills.

Her family was all legitimate now, or as legitimate as the super-wealthy ever were, but not through any choice of their own. Instead they had seen the pending abolition of slavery and had shifted their business model before its end had bankrupted them, as it had so many others. Her parents and grandparents had boasted of it as a symbol of the family's savviness.

What was she doing here?

What was she doing with Anton?

There was a strong possibility that her family's ships had delivered his ancestors into slavery.

Everything that had felt so light just moments ago disappeared beneath a shroud of wind-blown red dust.

CHAPTER 15

Anton didn't notice the change in Katie at first. He was simply glad that she'd rolled up her window to block out all the dust that had been getting on his nerves...though Hannah's was still down.

By the time they'd prowled this far along the twisting harbor streets and finally reached this faster stretch, the midmorning heat and humidity was making their dawn arrival feel like a Siberian memory. The sun thundered down on their rental so hard that the AC had crapped out and just left them to roast.

Like the gawking tourists they were, the others were pointing out interesting sights outside the car. At the moment they were focused on what Jesse's map declared were the *Deux Mamelles*—the two breasts—as the twin hills of Dakar were called. They weren't much, maybe a hundred meters each, but since the rest of the peninsula was under twenty meters, they stood out prominently. One was topped by a great white lighthouse and the other by a monstrous bronze sculpture that rose fifteen stories of a family questing for the horizon.

Glancing over for Katie's reaction, he'd seen her withdrawal.

He took her hand.

"Hey you." Real powerful opening line. He had to work on that. "What are you thinking?"

"Um, fairly vile thoughts actually." She didn't make it a joke with an easy smile.

"Not about me, I'm hoping."

"No. About my family."

"Huh," that had always been a hard one for him to answer. Sure, a lot of families sucked, he'd heard about more than his fair share in the service. But his didn't, so it was hard to really relate. "That bad?"

When she just nodded, he was even more at sea. For lack of anything better to do, he began toying with her fingers. Her whole hand barely covered his meat-hook palms, but they weren't delicate. Katie used her hands. They were good and strong.

"Want to tell me about them?"

"I'd rather never think about them again."

"Okay," he pulled her fingers apart enough to run a finger along the smooth webbing while he looked for a subject change. "You'll like my folks. They're just regular farmer types."

Again one of those strangely assessing looks.

Oh, dumb. So he turned it into a joke. "Look, if I'm going to put a ring on your finger, you're going to have to meet my folks. Just the way it works."

That earned him a pained smile. “If you’re lucky, you’ll never, ever meet mine.”

“Did they do shit to you?”

“Ow, hey,” she shook her hand, which he didn’t realize he’d clamped down on.

He eased off.

“No. They weren’t abusive. They…ignored me. I suppose they felt they needed an heir, reproduced, and then decided they couldn’t be bothered with the child.”

“What kind of a parent does shit like that to a kid?”

Katie studied his eyes for a long moment. Then, as if finding a surprise answer to his question, she spoke up.

“Chas.”

“Chas? That Chas Thorstad guy? What kind of a shit father would he be?”

“No, I mean—” Katie jerked her hand out of his like he was a branding iron or something. “Still there.”

She looked around desperately and Anton tried to see what had spooked her.

“Chas,” she said again.

He finally got it. She’d just felt him.

Even while she was telling Hannah to turn around, which looked to be completely impossible here, Anton dumped his vision out of the car and began running it back the way they’d come.

“Talk to me, Katie.”

“But I don’t feel anything until we turn around again.”

He probed around, reaching for her arm without bringing his vision back into the car until he found something soft.

"Hey!" By the angle that her hand took his, he suddenly realized what he'd taken a hold of.

"Oh God. I'm so sorry. I shouldn't have—" He hadn't just grabbed a woman's breast, had he?

"Warned you my big-little-semi-brother was too nice," Michelle chimed in happily.

Apparently he had.

Katie pushed his hand down against her thigh and then laid both of her hands over his to pin it there.

"I'm—"

"Shush," Katie whispered. "I'm concentrating."

He was trying not to concentrate on the feel of her athlete's thigh, or where his thumb overlapped her shorts and rubbed against the soft heat of her bare skin.

"Keep moving."

He found his focus again, mostly, and continued back the way they'd come as Hannah did whatever her driving tricks were. Without his vision to help him anticipate, it made him a little bit seasick as she slalomed the car back and forth, then carved a long turn around what he guessed to be a tight traffic circle. Or an illegal U-turn.

He swallowed hard and continued back up the road.

The highway here was two-lanes each way with a wide, knee-high concrete median; the same to either side. No traffic lights, no marked crossings. Pedestrians perched like sandpipers along the Carolina beach, dancing back and forth along the high-tide line—before spotting a brief break in the traffic. Then young and old alike jumped down to the roadway and raced to the median. Once clear of the first two lanes, they perched once more at the median, awaiting the tide of traffic racing from the other direction.

No one stopped.

"There! There!" Katie squeezed his hand urgently, drawing most of his attention back to her smooth thigh. He was getting seriously desperate to get his hands on this woman.

"Which way."

"How should I know?"

Duh! Her feeling didn't have direction without motion.

He walked his vision around a broad circle passing through a lane of traffic, two courtyards, and a stall selling potted plants. As he crossed a narrow dirt lane to the side, Katie called out, "Warmer!"

He hurried along the lane leading down between white- and yellow-painted courtyard walls. They'd been smoothed over with a slurry so that the concrete blocks didn't show, but as the whole city seemed to be made of the stuff, he assumed these were as well. It made all of the houses very angular. A curved wall was hard work with rectangular concrete blocks.

"Where are you?" Hannah asked in the car.

"I'm walking down a narrow dirt lane immediately after a plant-seller's stall."

"Shit!" Again he felt the car swerve. "I just passed that. A little warning next time, Anton."

"Yes, ma'am."

Katie didn't call out "cooler," so he kept heading down the road toward the beach, not that there were any other options.

When Hannah had finally found their way through the traffic again to where Anton was waiting, Katie couldn't help being charmed.

Hannah had said that greater Dakar had doubled in size in just twenty-five years and now was over a quarter of the country's population. It was easy to believe.

Yet here, just down from the towering white lighthouse, was a tiny enclave. A parking area big enough for only five or ten cars. A beautiful house on the left, a small restaurant with a wide, thatched porch perched on the cliff edge to the right. Between them lay a sweeping view of the sea a dozen meters below.

As none of the others had skills that would let them track Chas, they headed to the restaurant to order a late breakfast and wait. For the first time, perhaps the *very* first time, she and Anton were alone together.

Suddenly her worries about overlapping family histories, and her strange new role in the team, didn't seem so important. Now it was just the two of them on a lovely beach.

Unlike Cornwall, Dakar's waters were a dark blue that made the ocean's deep feel far more close and real. The rocky cliff and narrow strand of sand and boulder could have easily been Cornish, but the small sandy terraces covered by individual thatched roofs with no walls placed her firmly in the tropics for the first time in her life.

For just a moment, she let herself focus solely on walking along the sandy strand, holding Anton's hand.

At this hour, there were only a few people on the

beach and none under the thatched huts. To the south the beach opened up into a wider area and was dotted with umbrellas and a few lounges.

"You a one-piece gal or bikini type?" Anton rubbed his thumb over hers.

"One piece."

"Too bad. Bet you'd look amazing in a bikini."

"You'd rather I was naked."

"Damn straight."

Katie looked up at him in surprise. She'd been teasing, but he shrugged easily that it was truth.

Getting naked with Anton?

That image actually worked surprisingly well inside her head. Not that she was ready to tell him that.

A man as dark and tall as Anton, though much more slender, was playing with his dog in the low surf.

Except the big German shepherd wasn't playing, she was cowering. And the man had a heavy rope leash wound tightly in his fist.

"You don't think he's drowning that dog, do you?"

In answer to her question, Anton raised his hand in greeting.

The man waved back. He had a bright smile that made him look like he couldn't possibly be a foul dog-abuser. Over the years, she'd found more than one pet that she'd returned to a shelter rather than the owner—along with a vet's report of the abuse the animal had suffered.

"*Na nga def,*" he called out what sounded like a greeting.

"Hey there," Anton offered back.

The man tipped his head uncertainly.

"Bonjour," Katie tried French.

He lit up at that. When she asked if everything was okay, he'd responded with a whole tale of how Clovis was the only dog in the whole neighborhood who was afraid of the water. The seawater, which he was actively scrubbing into Clovis' coat as she cowered and the waves sprayed them both, was needed to kill fleas.

When he was done, he unclipped the leash, shooed the dog, and called out *At-cha.* "Get out of here." Clovis scrabbled for footing as another dog-high wave battered at them, then she scrambled for shore struggling over the wave-washed cobblestones toward the sand.

Katie waved and they continued down the beach searching for signs of Chas, when she heard the man call out loudly behind her—

"Attaque!"

Attack?

Katie spun to face the dog.

The speed of her motion must have triggered Anton.

However mild-mannered he might normally appear, he'd spun fast and low, gathering up a fist-sized rock even as he shoved her behind him. He was suddenly six-five of highly trained soldier on full alert.

The dog stood on the dry sand with her legs braced well apart.

Then she shook hard, creating a wide spray that caught the sunlight to make a brief rainbow. Katie managed to dodge aside, but Anton caught the brunt of the "attack."

"Désolé," the man apologized, but he was laughing, even slapping his thigh at the glorious joke.

The dog shook itself again, though the "attack" of seawater spray was far less on her second effort. Then the dog lay down on the sand to wait.

Anton was slow to rise to his feet. "I hope a goddamn wave flattens his ass."

"He said he was sorry." She waved and he waved back.

"Sorry my ass," Anton grumbled as he wiped the dog-water from his face. It took her some effort to control her own laughter as they headed once more along the beach.

They'd strolled another hundred meters or so when Katie had an idea.

"Hey, if he was local, do you think he knows where the cables come up?"

Anton just pointed.

A large sign was perched atop the low cliff another twenty meters ahead. The red lettering would have been weather-faded into unreadability if it hadn't been written so large. Though the pictogram of an anchor with a slash through it was something of a giveaway.

"What's it say?"

Katie had to squint to make out the faded French. "Cable Crossing. No anchoring."

"I think the cables come up right about…" he made a show of scanning up and down the beach, before pointing at the sign's base, "there."

"Jerk," but she squeezed his hand harder.

Then she felt him and shuddered for a moment.

"Chas was definitely here."

CHAPTER 16

They tracked back and forth across the beach.

"No. Just right here. Directly over the cables."

Anton watched her walk a quick circle around the narrow beach.

"One piece of it leads toward the parking lot. But in the other direction…" Katie stood at the edge of the water looking out to sea. "No, that's crazy."

"Try me," Anton edged up close behind her.

"There must be something wrong with my radar. Psychometric skills. Whatever you want to call them."

Anton indulged himself and wrapped his hands across her belly and pulled her back against his chest. She tucked as neatly under his chin as if she'd been designed to fit. "There's not a goddamn thing wrong with you."

"You're biased."

"Even if I wasn't—though gotta admit I seriously am—there's *nothing* wrong with you."

"Except I'm this weirdo freak with a psychic power."

"No!" His response was automatic. Instinctual. It hadn't required any thought.

Yet he'd said words like those a thousand times to himself. It hadn't bothered him; it had just been his sucky reality.

"No," he didn't care what he'd said in the past. "It makes you wonderful in more ways than you already are."

"Biased," but her voice was softer as she slipped her hands over the backs of his arms and leaned against him.

He could stand here like this all day, didn't care if the sun cooked him to a happy crisp. But he knew the others were waiting for them at the restaurant.

"What are you feeling?"

"Like if I don't get you into a bed in very short order, I'm going to melt with frustration."

"Okay, I can definitely work with that image. God *damn,* woman, can I ever. Except you said you felt something wrong."

"Boy scout."

"Eagle scout. Order of the Arrow."

"I should have known." He felt her sigh through his palms on her belly. "Chas—"

"Mood killer," he teased her.

"—went that way." And she pointed out to sea.

"Huh."

"Told you there was something broken with me. Bloody hell. Three days ago I didn't even know I had this power and now I'm convinced that I can tell the direction of flow. His trail gets…older…back toward the cliff. That direction is fresher sign."

He scanned the horizon. "No boats except some fisherman out past that point to the southeast."

"No, Anton. Look where I'm pointing."

He looked down at her arm, which pointed downward into the waves. "Really?"

Her shrug sketched twin lines of heat on his chest. Quite why that gave him an idea to do with anything other than getting this woman into a bed, he didn't know, but it did. Swimming?

"Want to try something weird?"

"Weirder than psycho-vision-localization of bad guys on different continents?"

"Yep." He figured this rated that—if it worked.

"I'll bet it doesn't involve that bedroom."

"Not yet. How about this instead?"

He stepped his vision out of his body and headed straight into the waves. The waves closed over him, but he could still see underwater.

"Are you okay?" Katie twisted enough in his arms to bang her head against his chin and click his teeth together.

He realized that he was gasping for breath, even though his body was still on dry land. It was a struggle to disconnect from what he was seeing and assure his body that it was fine, but he managed.

"Yeah, I'm fine. Just never tried walking underwater before."

"You think that Chas can walk underwater?"

"No. I'm thinking that he probably swam out from the shore, or was picked up by a boat. Maybe you can feel where he went from above or below. We'll have to test that someday."

Despite growing up within a few miles off the North Carolina beach, Anton had never dived, not even snorkeled. He knew how to swim and had survived egress training in the Army's dunk tank in case of a helicopter crash. Now he was following a sand slope downward.

Sun ripples painted the sand before him in sparkling light. An occasional fish swam by, one right through where his left arm would be if it wasn't wrapped around Katie's waist.

"Fish can't see me." He jumped when a rock he'd been circling around abruptly burst to life, leaving behind a cloud of black ink.

"What happened?"

"A little octopus and I just scared the ink out of each other. Guess *they* can see me."

"He's fading," Katie reported.

Anton zig-zagged until he picked up the right direction once more.

He hadn't really been counting steps, but he figured that he was roughly a kilometer offshore when he found the terminus of Chas' signal. No matter how he circled, Katie couldn't feel a thing except maybe a fading hint out to sea.

Then, in the dim light filtering down through a hundred meters of ocean, right at the center of Chas' disappearance, he found something grim that was all too easy to explain.

~

Katie poked at her Sicilian Citrus Scallops. She'd come all the way to Africa and chance had led them to an Italian restaurant. The chef, sick of the pressures of owning a restaurant in Rome, had come to Dakar. He'd built a restaurant with twelve tables that could seat barely forty people, and set about serving up southern Mediterranean cuisine.

The food was excellent. Her appetite wasn't.

In fact the only one who appeared to have a hearty appetite was Anton, presently devouring a deep bowl of fresh-made pasta with meatballs and red sauce. Maybe nothing bothered him. The other three military people were eating, if not as eagerly. Or maybe they'd seen so many worse things that this was mild.

She, Michelle, and Isobel hadn't really touched their food.

For her? Each time she thought she was surfacing and finding some new mental framework to handle what was happening to her, it collapsed. She couldn't actually *accept* any of it, but she'd been *managing* it.

Until Anton had walked beneath the ocean and found something.

"Are you sure about this?" Ricardo was looking unnerved. What did it take to unnerve a Delta Force operator? He'd shifted closer to Michelle when Anton had relayed the news. Protecting his wife was what had unnerved him. How must that feel to a warrior so used to operating on his own?

"Saw it with my own eyes. Didn't exactly have a camera."

He'd found one of the long Senegalese fishing boats,

resting on the bottom. Aboard were two fishermen with their necks broken, weighed down. Recently enough that the crabs had only just discovered the bodies. An anonymous tip to the police should recover the bodies for their families, but it wouldn't prove a thing about how they had died. Anton had concluded that the marks on their necks meant that Chas had done the deed with his bare hands.

The cool tile flooring and deep shade of the restaurant's thatched awning had nothing to do with the chill Katie felt prickling her skin. She'd been alone with Chas and the badgers. With a man who casually killed. She was lucky to be alive.

How close had Anton come to signing both of their death warrants when he'd plucked Chas from the ground to collect her guide's fee?

Rubbing her arms didn't drive away the goosebumps.

Ricardo's phone buzzed loudly enough against the wood table to make her jump.

While he inspected the message, Anton slipped his hand over hers. "It's okay, Katie. When it gets easier, that's when you have to be careful."

She looked up into his dark eyes. This was a different man. Not Mr. Easygoing. Not worried or amused. Katie felt like she was being offered a rare glimpse under the lid of the man Anton chose to present to the world. Inside was a quiet, thoughtful, intelligent man.

"What about you?"

His shrug was eloquent. "I try to compartmentalize. When I rescued Ricardo out of a Honduran hellhole, there wasn't a whole lot of the man that was intact. Body or…"

Anton tapped a big finger against his own temple. "With Michelle's help," like he was giving her extra respect by using her full name, "Ricardo found his way back. That's strong. If I can be even half that…" Again the expressive shrug.

She rubbed at her arms again, but the chill was fading.

"You're smart in ways I'll never understand, Katie. Like Missy."

The comparison surprised Katie. First, Michelle was incredibly smart, something Katie had never particularly felt despite earning good grades. But those grades had been her form of defense, to rise over the constant petty squabbles at boarding school.

The real surprise was that despite all of their verbal sparring, she could hear how much Anton loved his stepsister.

"But not like Isobel," she covered her nerves with the joke.

Anton understood of course and squeezed her hand to acknowledge it. "Ain't nobody smart like her." Then he continued more soberly. "I'm just a good helo pilot. Nothing like Jesse, but good enough. And I've got this… weird power. That's all." She could hear him shift away from the word "freak" but it felt as if he did it more for her sake than his own.

"You have one thing way beyond anyone here."

"Even Isobel?" he teased.

"Even Isobel." Katie shifted her hand so that they were clasped. "You are the kindest person I've ever met."

When he leaned down to kiss her, she wondered quite where this trail was going to lead her. For the first time in a long while, she was looking forward to finding out.

After the kiss, and her heartrate dropping enough for her to function, she picked up her fork with her free hand. It was the wrong one, but she didn't want to let go of Anton's grasp. She managed to spear a scallop and eat it without too much trouble.

CHAPTER 17

Anton wondered what the hell was happening to him. He liked women. Liked the way it felt to touch them, even when it was just holding hands.

Holding hands with Katie made him feel like an amateur.

For the first time, he was aware of everything. The softness and warmth of her skin, the strength of the muscles beneath. And her sweetly soft kiss! Damn but she had a mouth on her that he could spend a long time getting to know.

Ricardo cleared his throat.

Anton tried to ignore him as he studied the honey in Katie's amber eyes. They had darkened as she looked at him. He was just leaning forward to try another kiss when Michelle's elbow—she had seriously sharp elbows he'd know anywhere—caught him in the ribs.

She did it hard enough that he klonked foreheads with Katie hard enough to hurt and elicit a yelp of surprise from Katie.

"What?" Anton spun on Michelle.

Michelle tipped her head toward Ricardo at the other end of the table.

"What?"

"Now that I have your attention." To her other side, Ricardo offered one of his rare smiles, which was the height of a tease for a Delta operator.

"Should have left your ass in the jungle where I found it," Anton grumbled at him.

"Are you planning to hold that over my head for the rest of my life?"

"I figure it's got to be good for something. So, yeah."

They traded friendly scowls. There was a reason he liked Ricardo like a brother, even before he'd married Michelle.

"What have you got?" Anton decided to give him this round.

"The colonel scared up footage of a trawler *Kura* in the vicinity of where you found the fishing boat. We have no record of it, but it looks like it could be Russian."

"Means Chas is gone." At least they were done with that.

"No," Ricardo tapped his finger against his phone. "The *Kura* is still in the area. And she's got a crane big enough for launching a remote-controlled submersible. Wouldn't be hard for them to tap or sabotage the cable."

Anton took another bite of meatball and chewed on that for a moment. "If I was the Russians, I'd go for tapping it. This 2Africa cable is supposed to connect like twenty-something countries to the UK and a couple of the other Europeans. Bet Russia resents not being a part of that. If I was them, I'd mess with it."

"Why not do it in Cornwall?"

Anton didn't have a good answer to that one.

Michelle toyed with her spaghetti carbonara. "You said that the UK sites were really well protected."

"Except for Ricardo and Hannah messing with their heads at Skewjack, sure."

"What kind of protection do they have here?"

Anton didn't have the answer to that, but he knew where to look.

He ducked back to where he'd been holding Katie on the beach. The memory of holding her body close was very distracting, but he shook it off. Instead of walking into the ocean, he turned inland. Somewhere ahead of him was the cable landing point, but where?

At Sennen Cove it had been a farmhouse that wasn't actually in use. In Porthcurno, he'd found it on the lower floor of an unusually robust lifeguard hut. The four heavy manhole covers with secure locks, arranged in a line fifty meters from the hut, had been the giveaway there.

He started toward the cliffs when Katie whispered to him back in the restaurant. "His trail is fading."

He veered toward the wider resort beach to the south.

"That's better."

He upped to a jog, and with only a few corrections, he was soon standing by a brand-new one-story concrete-block house...with tinted windows. In the First World, it was easy to imagine some rich idiot installing one-way windows between themselves and the view. A glance to the side showed that not even the slightly sad excuse for a beach resort had any tinted glass.

He stepped through a wall into the dim interior.

Several heavy sea cables came up through the floor from the east—not much thicker than Katie's wrist. On the other side of the room, much lighter land cables, without all the protective layers and wrappings required to survive under the ocean, headed out through the floor to the west. The two sets of cables were joined together in a big equipment rack. It was the only furnishing in the entire house other than a large backup generator.

And in the midst of it all, was something that his Army training had been all too clear about.

"Shit!" Anton let the feel of Katie's hand slide him back into his own body. She made it effortless.

Ricardo raised his eyebrows in question.

"I was wrong about the tapping. How are you at disarming IEDs? This one looks nastier than any roadside box I ever saw in the Dustbowl."

"This is getting way too real," Katie whispered to Michelle as they sat on the beach, supposedly looking out to sea. A few hundred meters out, fisherman were pulling nets out of the water along a low headland. Pleasure boats didn't seem to really happen here.

"Are you talking about the Russians or my dram-brother?"

"I was talking about the Russians."

"Too bad," Michelle sighed. "I was hoping for a distraction."

Katie couldn't blame her. At this moment, Ricardo and Hannah were breaking into the cable hut to disarm the IED.

Anton had spotted two booby traps. A simple one on the door and a not so simple one that probably listened for radios and cellphone signals.

To bypass the latter one, Ricardo and Michelle were using their telepathic link to communicate. Jesse was outside the hut on lookout, to make sure they weren't interrupted, and hopefully to clear the immediate area if anything went wrong.

Out on the beach, Isobel had their team leader, Colonel Gibson, and a specialist in Russian munitions on the phone. Michelle was the relay between Isobel and the team infiltrating the hut. And Katie was the useless third wheel.

Katie held Anton's hand, not because she could help but because she needed to. They already knew that Chas, or whatever his actual Russian name was, had been there.

Anton kept his vision inside the house as a third set of eyes.

She hurt for Michelle. If the bomb went off, it would kill Ricardo and Hannah, but Anton would still be safe.

Michelle was methodically sifting the coarse sand through her fingers and slowly sorting the light grains and the dark into tiny piles.

As a test, Katie squeezed Anton's hand lightly. When he didn't squeeze back, she hoped that he was too focused to overhear.

"You have a weird relationship with your stepbrother."

Michelle sighed. "I have a weird relationship with everybody. My best friend is an international movie star. I married her brother, which is definitely a little strange. My husband, who I love to death—oh shit, I didn't just say that—can't put more than three words together in a row, even telepathically. His best friend is my stupid stepbrother, making the whole circle practically incestuous. If he and Isobel had gotten together, I was going to totally lose it. It's actually a relief that he's fallen in love with you."

Between one breath and the next, Michelle began relaying questions and instructions between Ricardo telepathically and the experts that Isobel had on the phone. They must have gotten safely past the booby traps. That at least was a relief.

But it was the only thing that was.

Katie was now the one having trouble breathing.

She liked Anton. A great deal. A whopping great deal.

And there was no questioning the electric charge that sizzled at the lightest contact between their bodies. She'd never so wanted to take a man to bed.

Falling in love with?

No, he wasn't doing that. And neither was she. Not a chance. This would be done and he'd be gone. No matter what they said, she'd only be part of their Shadow Force team as long as she was useful. If life had taught her anything, it was that she could only rely on herself. Others always—

"Where was I?" Michelle seemed to be done. Her expression looked even more stressed.

"How are they doing?"

"How would I know? I was in dress sales for most of my career. The whole paramedic, married-to-a-Delta-Force-soldier, Shadow Force: Psi thing is completely recent. I'm so lost."

Katie couldn't believe that the supremely confident Michelle was anything other than that. With her free hand, Katie took Michelle's gritty, fine-fingered hand. Michelle's grip crushed down on hers in desperate relief.

Katie held on tight. "You were telling me how relieved you were that anyone would want your stepbrother."

"What?" Michelle shook her head as if shedding some layer of the fear that threatened to overwhelm her.

"You teased me about your brother falling in love, even with someone like me."

"No. Fall*en* in love. He's already there but doesn't know it yet. I want to tell him just to, you know, freak him out, but I don't want to spoil his fun. You haven't decided yet, but you're close."

"Not bloody likely. What, are you suddenly an empath like Isobel now?"

"No," Isobel joined the conversation, "but it is rather obvious. And Michelle's right. It's lovely to watch you two. It gives me hope that I'll find the right man someday."

"But... but..." Katie knew she was spluttering. "You're Isobel Manella. You could have anybody you wanted."

"Show me a man who *doesn't* see me as that 'film babe,' and maybe I'll have a chance. And another actor," she shuddered. "That's a world of trouble I want no part of. Add to that, between acting and Shadow Force, my life is itinerant at best. Even nomadic. I'm never in one place more than few weeks, sometimes just for a few days. How am I supposed to have a family like that? Have a life? I sometimes wish I didn't love the acting so much. But my career is in a place where I keep getting offered better and better roles. The money has gotten so big that it's meaningless now, but I love the acting."

Isobel huffed out a hard breath.

"Sorry, it just catches up with me sometimes. Truly, it is so perfect watching you two find each other."

Michelle bumped a sympathetic shoulder against Isobel's before turning back to Katie. "Ma and Pa will love you, too. You're so…exotic."

"Exotic? I'm English. The English are never exotic."

"Your accent is so lovely that it will be, especially to a couple of North Carolina farmers. But if you love their son, they'll love you to death just for that. They think the world of Anton. Me? They love me, but I confuse them."

Katie got all set to protest but another round of questions arrived telepathically and Michelle and Isobel were focused on that.

She carefully glanced up at Anton.

His gaze was fixed out to sea. His stillness was absolute. Total focus.

Falling in love with a psi-powered American soldier who was a head taller than she was?

Why didn't the idea sound as unlikely as it was?

CHAPTER 18

"They got it." Anton heard Michelle's pronouncement echo his own.

Michelle's sob of relief snapped his attention back to the beach.

He kept his vision in the house just long enough to see Ricardo and Hannah gather up the explosives and their toolkit, and slip safely out of the building. Once they joined up with Jesse and were headed to the beach, he let his vision go.

He sagged against Katie as if he'd just run a marathon. He'd never watched a bomb being disarmed before. Watching it be disarmed by two friends who would be killed instantly if anything went wrong was terrifying.

When they arrived, Michelle leapt to her feet, raced to Ricardo, and wrapped herself around him.

"Shit! I should have thought about how hard this would be on her."

"Isobel and I were here for her."

He kissed her on top of the head and wrapped an arm around her shoulders to hold her tight. "You okay?"

"I was lucky. I knew you couldn't be hurt if it…went wrong. So it was only incredibly stressful instead of impossible. Your stepsister's an amazing woman."

"Yeah, I know." And he loved that Katie got that. Michelle needed friends like Katie in her life. "She was always a train wreck as a kid. Trying to be someone different every time you turned around."

"She said she was confusing to your parents as a child."

"Not half as confusing as she was to herself. But she's good with Ricardo. Really good."

"And who are you good with?" Katie suddenly blushed almost as red as Michelle occasionally did.

"You." It came out as if it was the truth. Then he realized that it was. He was already better just for being with Katie. He no longer felt like such a freak. She didn't mind that he could send his vision lookabout, didn't find him creepy or repulsive.

For just a moment he stepped back and looked at the two of them. That couple over there. Sitting on an exotic African beach. He had his arm around her shoulders and her arm had slipped around his waist without him noticing, because it felt so natural.

"Definitely you."

He slipped back into his body so that he'd be fully there when he kissed her.

Before he could, a heavy pack dropped to the ground at his feet.

He didn't need to look inside to know that it was filled with Russian explosives.

"Shit, Ricardo. Busy here."

"Get busy later. According to the timer we disarmed, in two hours, Chas is going to know that his sabotage didn't work. He'll either try again, or he'll tackle some other section of the cable and we won't know where. If he's determined to destroy it, we need to find a way to stop him sooner rather than later. And find out who's behind him."

"Shit, man. When does a dude get a break?"

"Back side of never," he echoed Ricardo's answer. He'd heard it often enough. During Ricardo's recovery from his torture in the Honduran jungle, he'd shut out Michelle and his own sister, Isobel.

Anton had figured since he'd flown in and hauled Ricardo's sorry ass out of the trees that such rules didn't apply to him. Besides, he'd been in the hospital with the hole in his leg that the rescue had earned him. So, he'd made sure to stay in Ricardo's face for all nine months of his recovery and physical therapy. There were some levels of trust that civilians could never understand…and the two of them had that.

Which meant if Ricardo said it was time to move, then it was time to move.

"So, what's the next play?"

Ricardo looked out to sea. "He's out there somewhere. Gibson is trying for some satellite time, but the Senegalese coast isn't exactly a hotspot we watch closely. A boat, maybe a couple of them?"

Jesse had dropped onto the sand with Hannah sitting between his knees. He was giving her a shoulder massage.

Anton had to remember to try that on Katie and see how it went. Hannah was sure looking happy.

"Be nice if we had a helo," Jesse sighed.

"Damn. That's why you made it to the Night Stalkers. You're so damn smart. Okay, genius. Where do we get one in Senegal?"

"Yellow pages?"

Hannah pulled out her phone, ran a quick search, then shook her head.

"There *are* two airports," Katie said softly.

"I'm listening."

"You know how new the commercial airport is, the one we just came through?"

"Uh-huh."

"Well, before that, commercial flights shared an airport with the military."

He exchanged a grin with Jesse. Military helos? Now they were talking. "Where is this old airport? Is the military still there?"

"I spotted the end of the runway when you sent Hannah driving in the wrong direction. It's a couple hundred meters that way," she pointed to the north.

Anton simply couldn't believe how amazing she was.

"And people ask why I love this woman." He swept her into his lap, and whispered, "I'm just plumb crazy about you." And ignoring Ricardo's groan of impatience, he kissed the crap out of Katie.

Katie wanted to resist.

Wanted to push back from Anton.

Take even a moment to consider his words. To wonder if he was even conscious of what he'd just said.

But his effortless strength had swept her up as if she was a fox kit. And his kiss was a toe-curler that allowed no other thoughts. All she could do was hold on and enjoy.

In moments, her head was spinning and she considered pushing him down to the sand right now no matter who was watching. Which wasn't like her at all.

She was just deciding that she didn't care who it was like, when Anton broke off the kiss. He crushed her to his chest and spoke to the others.

"So, how do we get a military bird?"

Katie couldn't even make sense of the words. They were closer to making love sitting clothed on a beach than she usually managed naked in a bed with a man. She liked sex, but with Anton, mere sex was already behind them. Even if they hadn't done it yet. He was— They were— She was—going insane!

"Can't get their help. If this gets ugly, Senegal needs to have complete deniability," Ricardo announced.

"Then we'll just borrow one," Anton sounded as if stealing a military helicopter from a friendly foreign power was going to be fun.

It should be the most ridiculous thing Katie had heard in the last forty-eight hours, but it wasn't. Instead, it made a strange sense.

"We need to get me and Jesse aboard. Be stupid if we don't have Ricardo and maybe Hannah with us."

"At least with your looks, you can pass," Michelle told Anton. "What about the other three?"

"Anton is giving some visiting American forces a military tour?" Isobel asked.

Katie wasn't the only one who looked at her in surprise.

"What? It would work as a movie plot. We just need some military uniforms and valid ID." To prove her point, she pulled out her phone and was soon talking to Colonel Gibson.

"Only see one problem, dim-demi-brother."

"What's that, Missy?"

"You don't speak Wolof or French."

"Well, you're not going, even if you do speak French. No way could we pass off five-ten of beautiful redhead as military."

Michelle slapped both hands to her chest and flopped onto the sand. "Oh my God! Anton called me beautiful. I can die happily now."

"Twit," Anton grumbled out.

"Jerk," Michelle replied, still prone on the sand.

"Love you too, Missy."

She sat up and kissed him on the shoulder before asking, "Who else speaks French?"

Katie was the only one who raised her hand.

"That doesn't help. We need the leader to speak the language."

That earned a glum silence.

Isobel finished her arrangements with Gibson and gave them a thumbs up.

But that still didn't solve the language problem.

None of them spoke Wolof.

Only she and Michelle spoke French.

The only other language the locals spoke was…

She started laughing. She'd finally found an idea that was crazy even by today's standards.

CHAPTER 19

Anton sat in the "borrowed" car at the rear security gate of Léopold Sédar Senghor International Airport. They'd borrowed it from a French ex-pat that the American embassy happened to know was presently in France.

"This had better work," he mumbled to Ricardo as the guard came over to check their IDs. If he spent the rest of his life in some Senegalese prison, it was going to be damned hard to make love with Katie.

"Katie's smart. I'm betting she's right. We'll know soon enough."

The guard came up and saluted sharply. The HK G3 battle rifle over his shoulder might be ancient, but it looked well maintained and well used.

Anton did his best to return the salute in an identical gesture.

The guard babbled something. The only word he could pick out was a French roll on *colonel.* He'd just go with assuming it was a greeting, as that was the rank on his "borrowed" uniform. In this case borrowed from a secret stash at the American embassy.

"Do you speak English, soldier?"

"Yes. A little."

"Good. Keep practicing. I will help you today by only using English. I'm Colonel Anton..." he hadn't been able to use Bowman on his fake ID. Some spook at the embassy had chosen a name for him, but what was it? Then he spotted the sign on the front gate and remembered. "...Senghor."

The guard snapped to attention. Senghor had been the first president after independence and—as the spook had promised—his extended family made it still a name to conjure respect with. For once the CIA had gotten it right.

"I'm giving these three American officers a tour. They're part of a surprise military aid investigation team. So don't warn anybody. They want to see with their own eyes how prepared we are."

The guard had enough English that he nodded his head in agreement. But he did inspect everyone else's phony IDs carefully. No surprise at having Hannah along.

Then Anton spotted the backup guard watching them from the far side of the barrier and it made sense. The Senegalese Army was integrated already. Hannah would be a surprise for her light skin and blonde hair, but no more than Jesse would be. Her gender didn't enter into the equation.

In moments they were rolling through the gates.

"Well, that's a start."

Coming in the southern gate had placed them close by

the helo hangars. The few Senegalese jets and cargo planes were on the other side of the field.

They rolled along the hangars and the sight was disappointing. Three small training helos didn't even have their rotors mounted. Two others had the rotors, but the flat tires said that they hadn't flown in some time.

Approaching the hangars was more promising.

A Bell 206 JetRanger would do.

A bulbous-nosed French Alouette III looked serviceable despite being at least forty years old. Better than one of the little prehistoric Russian Mi-2 Hoplites.

At the end of the row, there was—

"Oh, baby! Jesse, buddy, tell me we can figure out how to fly that sweet thing."

Jesse's slow smile was very promising.

It was an Mi-35 "Monsoon", the export version of the Russian Mi-24 "Hind" gunship.

It was big, damn big. Sixty-five feet of death.

Actually, it was almost exactly the same length as the Black Hawk that he'd flown for the Army, but there the similarities ended.

Instead of the solid utilitarian look of the UH-60, it was more like an Apache attack helo on steroids—lean and nasty. It could carry half the troops of the Black Hawk, but more weaponry than even a Night Stalkers DAP Hawk. The two stub wings to either side could have missiles, machine guns, or rocket launchers hanging from them, though they were bare at the moment.

Rather than side by side, the pilot and gunner sat front to back. The pilot perched beneath a small bubble canopy in the very bow, no wider than a cockpit seat and the controls. Behind and half a meter higher, the gunner perched under a canopy of his own.

Under the pilot's feet hung a chin-mounted 12.7 mm four-barrel Gatling gun. The jutting gun gave the already nasty machine a vicious-looking lower nose—like it was part scorpion.

No one was around. Anton checked his watch and decided that it must be time for the midday meal.

Anton looked longingly at the heavy weaponry stored along the hangar's walls, but remounting it was something they didn't have the skills for, or time to figure out. He did figure out how to check the bow gun and see that it had rounds. There were additional guns integrated into the fuselage, but he didn't bother checking them out. If he needed to fire them, he'd find out then if they were loaded. If they weren't, there was nothing he could do about it now.

"We've got fuel," Jesse reported as he climbed into the pilot's seat.

Anton climbed in as copilot behind him. He wasn't sure how, but Jesse had the rotors spinning in under a minute and up to a hard thrum in two despite all of the instrument markings being in French.

Anton got the intercom working as much by luck as guessing. Ricardo reported that he and Hannah were both aboard.

As Jesse was taking them aloft, a mechanic came out of a shadowed hangar and inspected them curiously. Anton saluted, and the man saluted back.

So far so good.

Then he turned and raced away, apparently calling the alarm.

The radio squawked with something. It must have been left on the tower frequency.

"Do something about that," Jesse called over the intercom.

"Don't bother. Ground crew are already raising the alarm."

"Try."

Anton tapped a thumb on the Mic button. Apparently the word "microphone" had come out of the French.

"Senegal Tower, this is Colonel Anton Senghor. I'm taking a…Canadian inspection team on a brief flight. Acknowledge."

Another spate of French came back at him.

"As a courtesy to our guests, I am only using English today."

"You have no filed flight plan. You have no flight authorization," the tower official sounded more frustrated than upset. That was a good sign.

"We'll be back shortly. We'll stay low and out over the water so there is no need to worry about interference with other flights."

"But—"

"Over and out, Tower." He tried for the command voice that his old flight leader used.

Only silence followed.

"Well, that's right peaceable, now, isn't it?" Jesse asked calmly.

"I guess. Unless they're scrambling fighters aloft to

shoot our asses." Just to save himself any future pain, he shut down the Tower frequency.

"Can't say as I saw much in the way of fighters. Those are a luxury to most small African countries."

"Here's hoping. Any signs of the trawler?"

"I see a lot of small fishing boats, but not much else. It's been hours, he could be anywhere in hundreds of square kilometers of ocean. This could take some time."

Anton found the fuel gauges. They had fuel, just not a lot of it. Time wasn't a luxury they could afford.

"Ricardo? You still online?"

"Yes."

"A man of many words. Use that telepathy of yours to ask around and see if anyone has any brilliant ideas on how we can find this bastard fast."

He started trying to figure out the weapons systems.

His first observation was there were a lot of them. He had sighting scopes, selectors, and triggers galore. But the only word he recognized on anything was "missile" which must be the same in French. It was a pity that he already knew there were none of those aboard.

"Shit! You'd think that Spanish and English would be enough for anyone."

"Texan is the real English," Jesse had them out to sea and was starting to sweep a long arc around the peninsula. "None of y'all speak a language that sounds like proper English a'tall."

"I'll see your Texan and raise you one Katie. That sweet accent of hers is how English is supposed to be."

"I may have to give you that point, pard. She does

make it sound jes' fine. Not like my Hannah's ever-so-smooth Tennessee, but still fine."

There was a click-thunk over his headset as Hannah must have keyed her mic switch in response. Sounded just like a quick kiss the way she did it.

"We have a suggestion," Ricardo reported.

The back of Anton's gunner seat had a small alleyway behind it. He didn't know what use it could be, his seat's back almost completely blocked the area, but it did lead into the cargo bay.

From that alleyway, Ricardo reached forward around either side of Anton's seat back, and clamped a hand on both of Anton's shoulders.

"That's an idea?"

Ricardo spoke to Jesse, "Fly us over Anton's underwater trail. Not too fast."

Anton still didn't know what to think as Jesse headed them that way.

"This is strange," Katie said for about the tenth time. The late afternoon light was driving straight on the beach. She, Michelle, and Isobel had returned there, below the cable house, for a lack of anywhere better to go.

"Just hush." She and Michelle sat hip to hip with their arms around each other.

A group of drummers had taken over one of the thatched huts back along the beach. The music and occasional laughter filtered their way. In the other direction, the area in front of the resort was also coming to life. Speakers blared out what seemed to be French rap. A buffet line had been set up and the guests were making use of it then returning to their loungers to eat and watch the sunset.

No sign of the thin man and his "attacking" wet dog.

"Why are we doing this again?"

"A while back, Ricardo and I used this for Hannah and Jesse. You know how one of them is the sound amplifier for the other?"

Katie nodded careful assent; she still hadn't seen that demonstrated.

"Well, they have to be touching to make that work. We were on a mission where they were apart and lives depended on them being together. Ricardo held Hannah and I hung onto that big old cowboy—which was a real hardship, I can assure you." Michelle winked broadly. "We kinda made some sort of weird conduit for them to connect. We're wondering if the same thing could work for you and Anton."

Isobel pointed aloft at where the big helicopter came pounding into view around the western point of Dakar.

"That is the most dangerous looking helicopter I've ever seen." Katie wanted to ask if that was really Anton and Jesse up their flying such a machine, but felt too foolish to ask.

The massive bird slid down until it was flying less than ten meters above the waves.

The fear caught in her throat. "Does he have to fly so low?" He was skimming the water like a petrel.

"According to Anton, that's Jesse's 'nervous' height.

Once he gets used to it, then you'll see him fly seriously low."

Katie tried to see if Michelle was teasing her or not when she felt a jolt.

"There. That was Chas' track."

Michelle was silent for a moment, then said, "We have a winner," in a tone so like Anton's that she must be transferring the message from Ricardo.

It was very different guiding the helicopter than guiding Anton. At first she sent it zig-zagging across the sky like a drunken pinball machine. But she soon had a feel for it—and the helo headed out to sea.

"What happens if they get too far away?"

"Oh, Ricardo and I can do this anywhere. The first time I ever heard him I was in San Antonio and he was in Honduras." Her sudden shiver said that it hadn't been a good memory.

They tweaked the guidance to the helo a little as it faded to a black dot. Then between one eyeblink and the next it seemed to merge with the bright horizon.

Katie could easily imagine in her future years, retelling her first meeting with Anton, her first in-person meeting. Chas Thorstad abruptly dangling half a meter in the air would open the story of "How mommy and daddy met." It would—

"Oh my God."

"What?" Michelle and Isobel asked in alarm.

"Nothing. Nothing. Nothing!"

"She's repeating herself," Michelle announced happily, sitting on her bottom and stomping her feet in the sand.

Isobel hugged her from the side opposite Michelle.

"No! No! No! I didn't just think that."

"Still repeating herself," Michelle was entirely too pleased.

Isobel was grinning like a fool. "Was it a wedding thought? Or a family one? Kids?"

"Kids. Bloody hell! I didn't just say that. Why don't you already know that?"

"I have empathy, not telepathy. So I can detect emotion, not thoughts."

"I did not—"

"Classic denial," Michelle practically crowed. "That cements it. Woo-hoo! There's gonna be a wedding soon! I'll fight Isobel to be your maid of honor."

"I think you'll have to fight Hannah." Again the world spun around Katie, but the words slid out anyway.

"Oh. She's a former Delta operator. I could put Isobel in the dirt—"

"Dare you to try," Isobel growled out.

"—but Hannah is tough."

"There's— They just flew past the trawler's track. It must have turned."

"No..." Michelle was gazing into the distance. "They just overflew the trawler itself."

"Oh God. Tell them to be careful."

CHAPTER 20

"Any reaction?" Anton asked over the intercom.

Ricardo still held onto his shoulders.

Hannah was their eyes behind, with her head stuck out the cargo bay's side door.

"Movement on the bridge, but I'm guessing it's mostly binoculars at this point."

Anton considered the crazy daisy chain that they were already running, Katie in contact with Michelle, Michelle linked telepathically to Ricardo, and Ricardo conducting Katie's sensing ability to him as an extension. Then the back channel of his voice, Ricardo's telepathy, and Michelle speaking to Katie.

"Well, hell, what's one more step? Jesse, pard," he gave it the cowboy's long drawl. "Why don'tcha fly us up high over that thar little boat and we'll see what happens?"

"What are you—"

"Trust me."

Jesse swooped the bird around and punched them higher.

Anton slipped his vision out of his seat inside the helo until he was hanging on just outside the helo. He didn't look at himself, as that was always kind of unnerving.

Instead he focused on the trawler and tried to time the angle.

"Never tried anything like this." And no matter what his brain knew about him being safe aboard the Mi-35 helicopter, for his heart this was the toughest stunt he'd ever tried.

He waited until they were directly over the trawler. Then he "let go."

His vision plummeted toward the boat.

Every instinct told him he was about to die. He was going to splat onto the deck from a couple hundred meters up and that was going to be the end of him.

The acceleration sped him downward.

At least he couldn't hear the roaring of the wind, but that boat was getting bigger fast.

Katie could feel Chas Thorstad directly below the helicopter. Like a hotspot. Perhaps he was pacing back and forth on the boat, making a bigger…signal?

Suddenly that signal began getting stronger.

Fast!

Clearer and clearer!

As if the helicopter—and Anton—were diving down directly onto the boat.

"They're crashing! Chas must have shot them down."

When the connection to Anton snapped, it was like a hard kick to the head. The pain was blinding until she found relief in passing out.

CHAPTER 21

Anton's feet landed on the deck as easily as he landed on the floor beside his bed in the morning.

"You okay?" Ricardo asked.

"Sure. I just jumped my vision down to the boat. Seems to have worked. Any problems?"

Ricardo was silent for a long moment. "Proceed with reconnoiter, just hustle."

"Yes sir, Mr. Bossman." The fact that he'd outranked Ricardo when they were in the Army was something he didn't lord over the man…too often. Besides Ricardo and Isobel were both natural leaders far more than anyone else on the team.

He trotted up onto the bridge.

"Seven baddies. Some serious hardware. Looks like mostly small caliber AK-47 knockoffs. But they have a couple of heavy machine guns of a type I don't recognize."

"Need to brush up on your Russian weaponry."

"Not sure what it is, but it's not Russian." That earned him some silence. "No sign of Chas. Going exploring."

"Hustle, Anton."

He wondered what Ricardo wasn't telling him, but he figured it would be better if he trusted Ricardo's judgment on that at the moment.

He sprinted down ladders and through cargo spaces as fast as his vision would go. He found Chas by himself down in a cramped galley area.

A countdown timer rested on the table beside him, it had less than five minutes remaining—maybe that's what was worrying Ricardo.

Chas was talking to someone on a tablet computer. On his phone, he had a bank account pulled up on his screen —a Cayman Islands one. It had a pretty impressive balance.

Then Anton looked at the face on the tablet computer.

Didn't take a rocket scientist to figure out what was going on.

"He's a mercenary. Waiting for his payoff."

Anton flipped back up to the bridge of the boat.

He looked at the crew members. He hadn't really looked at their faces in the shadowed bridge before. Then he leaned in close to inspect their weapons. At least he knew who they were, even if he didn't know why.

Then he recalled something he'd seen down in the cargo spaces as he'd run through them. He ducked back down to make sure he hadn't imagined anything.

"Oh shit!"

He let the vision go and was once more seeing the view from the back seat of the Mi-35 Monsoon helo.

Ricardo's hands were no longer on his shoulders.

"What have we got?"

"We have seven very angry looking Chinese with 7.62- and 12.7-millimeter weaponry. They have a cargo hold with enough explosives to make a damn big hole in the ocean."

"Chinese? What in the name of Texas are they doing here?" Jesse had the helo circling ten klicks from the trawler.

Ricardo answered him. "The Chinese have invested massively in African infrastructure. They're gambling that as it grows from Third World to Developing Economy, the investment will be paid back a whole bunch of times over."

"So what's the catch?"

"The catch is 2Africa. This brand-new cable encircles the entire continent and ties them to the UK, Spain, France, and Italy. It connects African data and financial commerce to Europe, not China. Someone decided the solution was to destroy the cable stations to discourage the countries of Africa from signing on. And they've got the explosives to do it."

Then Anton looked down at the fuel gauges. "Uh, if we ever want to see dry land again, we'd better do something fast."

"How about the chin gun?"

"Against a ship? Best I can do is chew up the deck some. That ship is solid."

There was a long silence, and all Anton could do was watch the fuel gauge.

"We've got less than ninety seconds on the clock,"

Ricardo said quietly. He was always the cool, collected one. "Jesse? Can you put us directly over their deck in that amount of time?"

In answer, Jesse slewed the Mi-35 around hard and laid down the hammer. "I don't suppose that there's any point in reminding y'all that they have a lot of machine guns. Even this baby won't take kindly to having a lot of holes put in her."

"I have a little present I want to drop on their deck without breaking it." Then Ricardo was gone.

"Why doesn't this sound good?" Anton began trying settings randomly in hopes of finding the setting to fire the chin gun. "Ricardo, could you ask Katie what the words are for machine gun, chin gun, or bow gun? Any of those?"

"Not gonna happen. Busy here," and he was gone again.

"What the hell does that mean?"

Jesse grunted. "Don't know, but I'm with you. Sounds like a case of laryngitis at a hog calling contest. Not good. Not one little bit of good."

Jesse had been cutting a wide arc, and now Anton saw why. Damn but Night Stalkers were so cool.

The landing gear was up, and his belly couldn't be more than two meters off the wave tops. If they clipped a wave, they would eat the ocean hard a few hundredths of a second later.

But even under pressure, Jesse had thought to come in directly at the stern of the boat. People would naturally watch to the front and sides. It would require someone being on the ball to watch astern. Even then, they were unlikely to look so low for a helicopter moving at two hundred miles an hour.

Anton might have come up with the idea, given a few minutes, but even with ten years in a Black Hawk, there was no way he could fly this route.

"Time?" Ricardo asked.

Anton glanced at the radar and air speed. "Fifteen seconds."

He stopped looking for the chin gun. All he'd do if he found it now was alert the ship to their approach. He dialed in his best guess and watched the radar scroll down the last two kilometers.

"At mid-deck, go straight up, but not until you reach mid-deck," Ricardo called out.

"My but he is in a fussy mood, ain't he?"

"That he is," Anton did his best to copy Jesse's lazy drawl. It was a pact among pilots that you only showed panic after you were already dead. Any sooner was just embarrassing and a general waste of time.

"You'll have less than five seconds to climb," Ricardo continued with his string of cheery news.

Anton tried to turn enough to see what Ricardo and Hannah were up to back there, but couldn't get an angle down the narrow alley behind his seat.

Despite the pilot's pact, Anton hissed in a sharp breath as Jesse flew straight at the boat's stern.

Ten meters out, maybe more like five, Jesse carved a hard left, then reversed through a one-eighty to pass across the middle of the boat.

He hesitated half a second directly over the ship.

Bullets began glancing off their canopy windscreens.

Anton tried the trigger.

The chin gun barked to life.

It poured out a stream of rounds. The first burst went up into the rigging. But when Anton pushed the weapon's joystick forward, the rounds poured into the bridge.

"Bomb's away," Ricardo called.

Jesse climbed sharply, but Anton was able to hose the bridge for two full seconds, almost three thousand rounds.

"What bomb?" He asked his question as soon as the chin gun spun dry and he could hear himself think again.

Then he remembered the bomb that Ricardo and Hannah had removed from the Dakar beach house.

"We didn't have a trigger, so I reconnected their timer."

"Su-weet!" Anton loved this outfit. It had taken two Delta operators and a consultant almost half an hour to disarm the weapon. They'd rearmed it in less than a minute on a swerving helo. They were definitely his kind of people.

Anton dropped his vision down to the boat.

Too bad he couldn't tap Chas Thorstad on the shoulder and wish him goodbye.

But Anton wouldn't forget the face of the Chinese man on the screen, or the symbol for the social media network he ran.

Yes, the Chinese social media would be very upset about losing their chokehold on Africa.

Seconds later the deck blew downward amid a blinding flash of light.

Chas was thrown against the bulkhead. Injured, but conscious.

He had less than a second to recover before the effects reached the lower hold and triggered the rest of the explosive cargo.

Anton let go of his vision as it sheeted pure white.

The view from above was little different.

A blinding fireball shattered the ship from stem to stern.

When he could see again, there was nothing left on the surface bigger than a pea patch. The ship had simply been obliterated.

The shock wave tossed them hard, but Jesse had gotten them enough altitude that he'd had plenty of time to recover them from the hard tumble well before they plummeted into the ocean. Though that might have gotten a little closer than was really comfortable, they made it.

He shouted back to Ricardo.

"Woo-hoo! Tell the girls we're coming home."

CHAPTER 22

Katie had been woken to a blinding headache by the massive helicopter racing up to the beach, slowing sharply, and creating a small sandstorm as it settled nearby.

Anton and the others had trotted over from the helo, laughing as they came.

Even Ricardo had been smiling broadly as he called out, "Let's get moving, folks, The police and the Army are bound to be here soon to fetch their helicopter."

Before she could rise, Anton had simply scooped her against his chest and carried her away.

And now he looked so perfect here on his family's North Carolina back porch steps. His elbows rested on the top step and his long legs reached all the way down to the grass. She sat a step down from the top, so that his fingers were sliding softly up and down her back.

"Nothing in the world like Ma's barbeque."

Katie would have to agree. Just as Michelle had predicted, Ma Bowman had loved her the moment she saw how happy Katie made her son. And she made an amazing pork barbeque.

The others looked equally content.

Beyond the gathering on the wide back lawn, the farm stretched away into the dusk. The air above the big kitchen garden to the right was a playground cluttered with swallows dancing through the evening light. A towering *Magnolia grandiflora* scented the night air with lemon, and a massive swamp white oak, *Quercus bicolor,* stood guard to the south. Between them lay the entrance to the fields and orchards.

Isobel sat with Anton's and Michelle's parents. Ricardo and Michelle were playing with an energetic yellow lab puppy. Jesse and Hannah sat arm in arm on the porch swing.

"You know what would make this perfect?" The effect of Anton's touch gave her a definite answer to that, but she wanted to see what his idea was.

"No."

Anton rose to his feet and held out a hand to help her to her feet. She was a little lightheaded from lack of sleep. They'd left Dakar behind within twenty-four hours of arriving.

It had also taken the headache hours to clear, even with the aspirin Michelle had given her. Whether it had been caused by the speed of Anton's "falling" away from her or the tag-team connection through Michelle and Ricardo's telepathy, she wasn't particularly interested in finding out. It would be a long time before she tried either one again.

But she didn't want the evening to end.

"It would be perfect if you were to take a walk with me."

Definitely not the quiet bedroom she'd been thinking of. They still hadn't made love, but she was too content to argue. Taking her hand, he led her at an easy stroll around the kitchen garden and out into a grove thick with magnolia trees and their heady scent.

"You know," Anton guided her around a set of beehives, "it just happens that I came into some money. I'm splitting it all ways with the team, which includes you."

"That's sweet of you."

"Yeah, I thought so too. Isobel doesn't need it of course, and is trying to refuse her share, but it's only fair."

Katie shuffled to a stop as the moon came out from behind a cloud and sent glittering shafts of light down through the trees.

Anton had given her so many gifts, including, some day, the gift of his family. She no longer doubted that the trail of her future lay alongside Anton's.

"Um, I don't really need the money either."

"Says the woman living with one change of clothes in her backpack."

"Two. I have two."

Anton leaned back against a tree trunk and pulled her against him. She didn't fight him a single inch of the way.

"I actually have a *lot* of money. I just never want to touch it." And she told him about her parents, her heritage, the slave ships. All of it.

He kept his silence through her whole story. By the end of it she began to worry. She didn't know how he'd react to her ancestors selling his ancestors. Or that her parents had been depositing a "paltry" ten thousand pounds a month into her account since she was four.

"That's a couple million pounds," was the first thing Anton said.

Katie froze. She'd been worried about the past history, but hadn't given a thought to the possibility of parents' money coming between them.

"Personally, I think you should take it."

"Why?" She asked the question very fearfully. If she had it, and they did marry, then he—

"Seems to this country boy that if you don't touch it, they win. Take their money, Katie. Do something with it. Buy a third change of clothes, buy a house. Doesn't really matter. Maybe find some way to use it that would make your parents nuttier than a Reese's Peanut Butter Cup. Seems like the least you can do for how they've treated you."

"That's…" Katie could only blink in surprise. Anton was never quite what she expected. And to turn that burden around, turn it into something *good?* Why hadn't she ever thought of that for herself? "That's unbelievably brilliant! I really love you."

"I love you, too, Katie," he brushed a hand along her cheek.

"Just like that?"

"Just like that."

She leaned her cheek against his chest and decided that he was right. Just like that.

"You could even just give all that money away if it bugs you. You'd still have plenty."

"How much money *did* you come into?"

"Four hundred thousand."

"Bloody hell." That was more than she'd made from tracking, ever. "Divided by the seven of us, that's almost sixty thousand apiece."

"No," he kissed the top of her head. "I came into four hundred, and so did you and all of the others. Each. I just might have seen Chas Thorstad's Cayman Islands bank account number before we sank his sorry ass. I cleaned him out this morning. Just before the Chinese cleaned out that billionaire jerk who bankrolled him."

"Four hundred..." She couldn't even imagine that much in a lump. And it meant that Anton had just given two-point-four million dollars to his friends as if he were handing out...slices of sweet potato pie like his mum was back at the house.

As if she needed even more proof of what a good man he was.

"Look," he whispered.

She looked up at him, blending into the darkness except for a few spatters of moonlight.

"No, out there."

She turned and the whole field under the magnolias was filled with fireflies flickering on and off.

"They're beautiful."

"Not half as beautiful as you, Katie Whitfield."

"Biased."

"Damn straight." He slipped his fingers down to her waist and tugged her shirt from her shorts. "Ever make love among the fireflies, Katie Whitfield?"

Unable to speak, she just shook her head.

"Let me *see* you, Katie."

She just raised her arms and let him slip off her blouse over her head.

Her trail had led her many places. She'd never imagined it would be to a place like this.

And now she didn't have to imagine it, because it was real.

She closed her eyes and leaned into Anton's touch. She knew that he could see the way ahead clear enough for both of them.

Be sure to keep reading to see an excerpt from the heart-warming conclusion to the series!

BE SURE YOU DON'T MISS...

THE CONCLUSION TO THE SERIES!

AT THE CLEAREST SENSATION (EXCERPT)

Isobel Manella stood at the end of her pier. Sadly, she was there in both the literal and metaphorical sense. The film actress in her appreciated the juxtaposition, but the woman she was didn't at all. Except it wasn't even a dramatic pier, it was just a little floating dock, and the crashing waves were inch-high wind ripples, rolling across the quiet urban lake to lap below her feet.

"What was I thinking?"

The gull bobbing gently nearby didn't answer back and she really, really wished it would.

Reflecting the Seattle skyline, Lake Union lay quiet beneath the summer sunset. The breeze rippled the surface just enough to break up the bright reflection of the lowering sun. It was hard to believe that she was in the heart of a major American city. Her home in San Antonio might boast the River Walk, but it had nothing like this.

The lake was a half-mile wide and a mile-and-a-half

long. The southern shore was protected from the urban core by a thin line of restaurants and a wooden boat museum. The expanse of a park filled the north end with a lovely grassy hill that caught the evening light.

To the east and west, tall hills rose steeply, thick with a piney green so verdant that it practically clogged the air with oxygen. Only scattered apartment blocks and low office buildings risked those slopes that resisted most attempts at urbanization.

On this quiet June Tuesday, the lake was thick with more sailboats than all of Canyon Lake on July 4th weekend. Every year, Mama had made a point of driving the forty miles from San Antonio to take her and Ricardo there for the parade and fireworks. After she'd died, they'd only gone one more time—to scatter her ashes where their father's had been all these years.

Isobel had never become attached to the sea; it was too vast and unruly. But she loved the happy bustle of a big lake.

The shoreline here was lined with marinas for boats of all sizes from daysailers to mega-yachts. Even a few massive workboats added their contrast to the scenery.

Several large houseboat communities also gathered along the shore. Though houseboats conjured the wrong image for her. A houseboat was a trailer on a rectangular metal hull rented for a few days on Canyon Lake. These were actual floating homes, hovering along finger piers that stuck out from the shore. They created a world away from the city, a quiet corner, without having to travel miles through sprawling suburbs to seek some peace. From here, the predominant evening sounds were the slapping of sails interrupted by the occasional hard burr of a seaplane lifting from the water.

No, the problem wasn't the lake. Or the "houseboat" she'd rented for the team. She turned to look at it, a pleasingly eclectic mix of old and new. The weathered cedar-shake siding was offset by the dramatically large windows.

It had four bedrooms, three baths, and a luxurious great room that spanned the entire first floor and made it easy for her team to all be together or spread out in smaller groups. It had an open plan kitchen that reminded her how much she used to enjoy cooking, back when she had the time.

The back deck had a rack of single and double kayaks. A smaller deck spanned across the two front bedrooms on the second story. And the rooftop deck was ideal for looking out over the lake to watch the sunset light up the sixty-story-high Space Needle even though the sun would soon be sliding off the lake and going behind Queen Anne hill.

She could happily stay here forever.

Another spatter of laughter sounded from the rooftop deck, which she could hear clearly from where she'd "reached the end of her dock."

The problem was her team.

Not that she didn't love them all.

But the other members of Shadow Force: Psi were now three couples. Her twin brother had married Isobel's best friend. They now supported each other more than her. She wouldn't wish it otherwise, but still she missed them—even though they were right …there, up on the roof. And her best friend's stepbrother had just become engaged to a lovely English lass. Even the quiet Hannah and her cowboy husband were utterly charming.

But she could *feel* their happiness.

She and Ricardo had grown up in a hard household. Papa dead in the Gulf War. Mama a single mother who'd run an entire nursing staff at a major hospital. Isobel had run their household from the time she could reach the stovetop from a stool.

They'd made it. A tight, hard-working unit. Then, while Isobel was in college and Ricardo in the Army, Mama was suddenly gone. Her death still left a hole in Isobel's heart that the last decade had proved would never heal.

By keeping her team close, she was surrounded by happiness every day.

Yet she wasn't just a third wheel to Ricardo and Michelle's happiness. She was now a seventh wheel to all three couples.

Shadow Force: Psi was between missions, so they'd all accompanied her here and were looking forward to helping on her latest film—with an excitement that was a little overwhelming. They'd arrived in Seattle just this morning and everyone had plunged into enjoying themselves as not a one of them had been here before. Nine years and a lifetime ago she'd been here to shoot her breakout rom-com but not been back since.

Isobel had been managing it, enjoying their sense of fun.

Until Michelle had announced that she was pregnant.

The general excitement had turned to near ecstatic joy.

Hannah had exchanged a look with Jesse, who then announced that they were going to start trying, too. Michelle had cried on Hannah's shoulder that she might not be facing this alone—as if that was possible in this group.

Isobel couldn't be happier for them...but her mind couldn't shut them out.

They each had their unique gifts. Some of them could switch them on and off, others couldn't. Michelle and Ricardo shared a telepathic link that was unique to them, and always worked without fail. Though Ricardo occasionally complained about being unable to shut out his wife's thoughts. The others had absolute control over their skills. Hannah and Jessie could do strange things with creating sounds, really strange and useful things if they were in physical contact. Michelle's stepbrother Anton could send his vision out to take a look around without having to drag his body along. And his fiancée Katie could feel if someone had been in a certain spot and then use her wilderness tracking skills to follow their trail.

Normally, her own empathic gift was wholly under her control. She could choose to sense what those around her were truly feeling, or she could shut them out and just be "normal."

It was a skill she'd always had, but hadn't known was unusual until Papa had been killed in action. Mama had put on the brave mask for her four-year-old children, but Isobel had been overwhelmed by that hidden grief. She'd had to learn at a very early age how to turn off her extra sense in order to survive.

But tonight the joy was so thick in the air, she hadn't been able to shut it out. She couldn't breathe.

"How can we stand it?" she asked the gull who had drifted to the other side of the dock.

Apparently deciding that she couldn't (or that Isobel was not being sufficiently forthcoming with some torn bread), the gull fluttered aloft and soared off in search of less frustrating places.

If only she could do the same.

Again happy laughter, big and deep this time. It sounded as if Michelle's stepbrother, Anton, had talked Katie into *all* of them trying to have their children close together even though their own wedding was a month off.

Isobel rubbed her own midriff.

She ached to be like them. Be one of them in this moment.

But all she could see of the future was becoming Auntie Isobel. Always cheering for others but never for herself.

Her face had been on every cover from *Vogue* to *The Hollywood Reporter* as her career had exploded. Even her Christmas blockbuster had busted the block beyond all projections. *People* had imaginatively dubbed her "The Sun-kissed Actress." No matter how non-PC it was to emphasize her skin color, it was true that fortune was absolutely smiling down on her. Amazing career. Incredible friends who truly understood the joys and fears of being gifted. A challenging life with the secretive Shadow Force.

And the personal life of a lone oyster. At least those lucky mollusks got pearls.

Every man who saw her, instantly thought he knew her—and wanted to conquer her. Not her, but rather her / the Movie Star. Her chances of finding what all of her friends were now up above celebrating, decreased with each passing film.

The evening was still bright, but soon the team would notice she was gone.

Michelle would come find her first; she knew Isobel's moods better than she did herself. She'd slip a friendly arm around Isobel's waist—her emotions thick with the green velvet of her core kindness, and rolling pink with compassion—and say something completely outrageous that would make her laugh and feel as if she belonged and was just being foolish.

Isobel didn't want to be consoled. She didn't want to live through her friends' relationships, through *their* children.

Since playing the "Crippled Girl" in *The Pied Piper of Hamlin* during second grade—a role she'd landed because her mother the nurse had been able to borrow a child-sized crutch from the hospital—she'd loved acting. But the price! The price was terribly high, and growing all the time.

She closed her eyes and concentrated on shutting herself off from others.

There was only her, the evening breeze, the warmth of the early evening sun on her face. She leaned toward its warmth. She could just—

"Don't do it!"

Isobel opened her eyes and looked at the man who'd called out to her. He floated a short way off in an elegant sailboat. It was long and lean, with a teak deck and a bright-varnished wooden hull. She'd never sailed on one, but she knew it was a model called a Dragon. It had been easy to remember because it was how sleek a flying serpent should look.

"Excuse me?"

"Don't jump, lady. Whatever's wrong, it's not worth it."

She looked down at the water lapping quietly a foot below her bare toes. One of the first things they'd all done on arrival this afternoon was jump into the water and swim about to wash off the flight from San Antonio.

"I *think* I'd survive the fall."

"Maybe there's a hungry Kraken lurking below. Why risk possible doom when you can sail?"

She focused on the man. His skin was roughly as dark as her own though differently toned—less Latin-brown, more desert ochre. Black hair strayed down to his collar and a close-trimmed beard and mustache emphasized the strong cheekbones that stood out despite his mirrored sunglasses. He wore denim cutoffs, and the edge of a colorful tattoo peeked out from the sleeve of a white t-shirt that declared, "I'd rather be sailing."

She nodded toward his t-shirt. "But you are sailing."

"Wouldn't *you* rather be sailing?"

"I'd rather be doing *anything*."

Keep reading at fine retailers everywhere:
At the Clearest Sensation

ABOUT THE AUTHOR

USA Today and Amazon #1 Bestseller M. L. "Matt" Buchman started writing on a flight south from Japan to ride his bicycle across the Australian Outback. Just part of a solo around-the-world trip that ultimately launched his writing career.

From the very beginning, his powerful female heroines insisted on putting character first, *then* a great adventure. He's since written over 60 action-adventure thrillers and military romantic suspense novels. And just for the fun of it: 100 short stories, and a fast-growing pile of read-by-author audiobooks.

Booklist says: "3X Top 10 of the Year." PW says: "Tom Clancy fans open to a strong female lead will clamor for more." His fans say: "I want more now...of everything." That his characters are even more insistent than his fans is a hoot.

As a 30-year project manager with a geophysics degree who has designed and built houses, flown and jumped out of planes, and solo-sailed a 50' ketch, he is awed by what is possible. More at: www.mlbuchman.com.

Other works by M. L. Buchman: *(* - also in audio)*

Thrillers

Dead Chef

One Chef!

Two Chef!

Miranda Chase

*Drone**

*Thunderbolt**

*Condor**

*Ghostrider**

Romantic Suspense

Delta Force

*Target Engaged**

*Heart Strike**

*Wild Justice**

*Midnight Trust**

Firehawks

MAIN FLIGHT

Pure Heat

Full Blaze

*Hot Point**

*Flash of Fire**

Wild Fire

SMOKEJUMPERS

*Wildfire at Dawn**

*Wildfire at Larch Creek**

*Wildfire on the Skagit**

The Night Stalkers

MAIN FLIGHT

The Night Is Mine

I Own the Dawn

Wait Until Dark

Take Over at Midnight

Light Up the Night

Bring On the Dusk

By Break of Day

AND THE NAVY

Christmas at Steel Beach

Christmas at Peleliu Cove

WHITE HOUSE HOLIDAY

*Daniel's Christmas**

*Frank's Independence Day**

*Peter's Christmas**

*Zachary's Christmas**

*Roy's Independence Day**

*Damien's Christmas**

5E

Target of the Heart

Target Lock on Love

Target of Mine

Target of One's Own

Shadow Force: Psi

*At the Slightest Sound**

*At the Quietest Word**

White House Protection Force

*Off the Leash**

*On Your Mark**

*In the Weeds**

Contemporary Romance

Eagle Cove

Return to Eagle Cove

Recipe for Eagle Cove

Longing for Eagle Cove

Keepsake for Eagle Cove

Henderson's Ranch

*Nathan's Big Sky**

*Big Sky, Loyal Heart**

*Big Sky Dog Whisperer**

Love Abroad

Heart of the Cotswolds: England

Path of Love: Cinque Terre, Italy

Other works by M. L. Buchman:

Contemporary Romance (cont)

Where Dreams

Where Dreams are Born
Where Dreams Reside
Where Dreams Are of Christmas
Where Dreams Unfold
Where Dreams Are Written

Science Fiction / Fantasy

Deities Anonymous

Cookbook from Hell: Reheated
Saviors 101

Single Titles

The Nara Reaction
Monk's Maze
the Me and Elsie Chronicles

Non-Fiction

Strategies for Success

Managing Your Inner Artist/Writer
Estate Planning for Authors
Character Voice

Short Story Series by M. L. Buchman:

Romantic Suspense

Delta Force

Delta Force

Firehawks

The Firehawks Lookouts
The Firehawks Hotshots
The Firebirds

The Night Stalkers

The Night Stalkers
The Night Stalkers 5E
The Night Stalkers CSAR
The Night Stalkers Wedding Stories

US Coast Guard

US Coast Guard

White House Protection Force

White House Protection Force

Contemporary Romance

Eagle Cove

Eagle Cove

Henderson's Ranch

Henderson's Ranch

Where Dreams

Where Dreams

Thrillers

Dead Chef

Dead Chef

Science Fiction / Fantasy

Deities Anonymous

Deities Anonymous

Other

The Future Night Stalkers
Single Titles

SIGN UP FOR M. L. BUCHMAN'S NEWSLETTER TODAY

and receive:
Release News
Free Short Stories
a Free Book

Get your free book today. Do it now.
free-book.mlbuchman.com

Printed in Great Britain
by Amazon

45538579R00130